A.M. FAZIO

This Side of Memory

This time for Beth,

My Sister and My Buddy

Indian Neck, Branford, CT

1969

Gina and Olivia sat around the playpen on the green shag carpet in the upstairs bedroom. “Look at that,” Gina said, a huge smile across her face.

“Yeah,” Olivia said, a similar smile as she brushed some of the curly hair from in front of the boy’s eyes. “Vincent and Isabella. Two peas in a pod. You’d never know that they weren’t related.”

Her smile changed to something more somber. It was a look that the twenty-three-year-old had seen a lot of lately.

“Rosalie would have been a great mother; God rest her soul.”

Both sisters quickly made the sign of the cross. Leaning forward on her knees, lifting Isabella, Gina simply stated. “We’ll just have to raise her as our own.”

Friday2008

1.

There was so much sadness and despair. Yet there was always much more happiness and warmth. The cold dark emptiness of the latest funeral was predictably dispelled by the comforting joy of the next wedding or birth. There were emotions here, and they came alive with every scent that triggered a memory and every sound that elicited a circumstance unique to its harmony.

The cottage was not just brick and wood, a fence, and a picnic table, although these things did have their place alongside the actors that played out their lives on this simple stage. The cottage was more, much more. It was life at its best and worst. It was yelling for accomplishment and screaming out into the universe during pain. Those that lived here were what brought life into this place. Some stayed longer than others, all with different reasons for coming and going, all leaving a part of what was themselves here, in this special place.

There were the musty curtains that once billowed with the fresh spring air. The hand-dug cellar that once housed a winter's supply of canned vegetables that was now only a home for small insects and time's dust.

But this place was once alive! I know this because I lived it. I was here. I was a part of these memories, a part of this place. Once upon a time the rooms literally sang with the excitement of Christmas and the New Year. Toasts flew heavenward, just as freely as the homemade wine poured into glasses that never really seemed to match. Children were brought to this place. They were brought here to be cared for and loved. These children grew up to be teenagers playing ball in the front yard or swimming at the beach that one could see from the cottage's East-facing window. They waited for the bells of the Good Humor truck on Saturdays and the bells of the Catholic Church each Sunday. The teens went off to work or war or college, but they always came back here. The cottage embraced them with familiarity, surrounded them with love or provided a final resting place after a life robustly lived.

They came back for anniversaries, holidays, vacation, funerals, weddings, and reunions. But they came back. That was what kept the small cottage alive. That's what kept those that did not go away full of hope and plans, dreams, and longings. But the cottage and those that lived within grew older. Somehow it happened that the newer families began to stay away. They moved out of state for work. They took husbands or wives that the rest of us had never met and had children that would call somewhere else home. And as their clean-shaven faces slowly grew hair that slowly turned grey, the cottage slowly turned quiet. None of us realized it at the time, but one day it had somehow lost its relevance as youth passed into adulthood and into old age.

It wasn't supposed to happen, and it wasn't intentional, but the next generation had cell phones and video games that interested them more than whiffle ball and playing Setback. They weren't interested in songs and stories of wars that took place before they were born. They had no time to sit and listen to stories about coming to this country, of dreams…they were too busy to dream, and wasn't this country theirs by default anyway?

The little cottage on the cove of Long Island Sound in a tiny Connecticut town could not contain them. It was quaint. It was where old people lived. They would rather be somewhere else.

But the cottage still stood! And I remember it, despite the many miles and many missed opportunities, I do still remember. It's my history, but more, it's where I find my sense of belonging.

2.

These thoughts and hundreds more came flooding back into my mind as I made the final turn into the cottage's gravel driveway and turned the engine off. I left the lights on and my SUV's door ajar as my fingers found the old key that would, as in time past, unlock the rusting bolts. The key was cold in my hand, but I took a moment to enjoy the sensation. It was a throwback to when the gate was new, and my hands had helped build the wooden fence that barred my entrance tonight. "Yes, I have part of me here," I thought, and smiling I turned the key and the lock disengaged with some resistance. It was almost as if the cottage knew I was here and more importantly, the reason why.

I opened the gate to its widest and climbed back into my SUV. The entrance was made for smaller cars in a smaller time, and I paused for a moment to exhale when I cleared the sides. I gathered my personal effects of a briefcase, day bag and a bag of fruit. One beep on my keychain reminded me that the SUV was both locked and foreign to this place.

I had always kept the electricity on here just in case. Thought it might help some wayward member of the family that was trying to find themselves by trying to find home. It was damp inside and dark, even with the meager lighting from a pair of 60-watt bulbs in orange porcelain lamps in the tiny foyer. I shuffled around, gently tossing my keys on the table and bags on the nearest chair, while quickly yet absentmindedly recalling how many times I and others had done the very same thing at different times. The keys landed solidly on the wooden table, an indention from a meat grinder still visible on the farthest side by the window. The sills were dusty, and the blinds showed age, or worse, abandonment. I pulled the screen door closed and locked it out of habit. The wood frame on wood jambs with the small latch wasn't designed to keep people out, but just to keep the door from opening and closing with the gusts of wind from off the Atlantic.

The night was cool, and the breeze was steady. After securing the screen door I intentionally left the main wooden door open. The salty night air cooled me and freshened the cottage. In my bag of fruit was also a quart of orange juice and in my day bag was a small bottle of gin. I took a rocks glass from the cabinet where I knew I'd find it and mixed the two. I drank one for myself, mixed another, and drank one for those who were here with me only in spirit. The slight burning of the warm liquor infused with the cold juice was a pleasant mix on this evening. I pulled my chair closer to the table and smiled to no one that was visible. The chair's wooden legs took my weight with a slight creak. As it had been for so many years, only three of the four legs touched the floor at any given time. My Uncle Giovanni who brought the chairs home from "a friend of mine" never was much of a carpenter, and certainly didn't compare to the cooking skills of his wife, Aunt Theresa.

Aunt Theresa's cooking! Gravies - we call them sauces now, with fresh Roma tomatoes cut right here at this table. Then we'd boil them down for hours with garlic, oregano, sausage, and oil. Stirred lovingly with that wooden spoon of hers, almost black from all the old flavorings it had absorbed throughout the years. Add a little wine. Add salt pork and some chicken. Roll the noodles out and let them dry over towels on a clothesline hanging on the porch. All were welcome! Bring your family, your friends, the kids down the street. There was always enough and more. There were meatballs frying in a pan after they had properly baked.

"How much salt?"

"A pinch."
"How much you wanna make?"
"Better too much than not enough."
"How much pepper?"
"Some. Joey coming tonight?"
"Yeah. With Rita."
"From the Church?"
"Si. Good girl. Italian. I know her mother."

3.

I opened my eyes. I had nodded off. What was this power that was here? What had I rediscovered? Had this tranquility always been here waiting for me to simply return? Of course it had. And much more. I leaned back and took a paring knife out of the small drawer to the left of the sink. It was the same knife my grandfather Nono and I used so many times so long ago as we waded in the cool water on the coral rocks in the cove. I sliced off a piece of apple that I had brought and wished for some cheddar cheese. I remembered the smell of the shore and the fresh clams and oysters.

My grandfather was such a jolly man. That's the only word that works for him. He was jolly. Silver hair receding from the front and his own band of broken English. We would look for oysters and clams at 6 a.m. on the small jetty that was just south of the cove. I was his only grandson, and I would follow along walking in his footsteps trying to pop open the mollusk shells with this knife I was now using to dissect the tasteless apple I had bought in a bag of fifteen or so - not freshly selected from a corner market as Nono had done.

The corner market was not there anymore, of course, falling victim to unregulated growth. The new Super-center carried everything the old corner market did and the thousands of products more, all for a lower price, faster service, and good dividends on their publicly traded stock. As I thought about the heavily waxed apples I had purchased, compared to the fresh apples hand selected by Mr. Bonezelli, the grocer, and brought home by my grandmother, Noni, I wondered if the price paid wasn't too great. There was at one time human contact. There was pride in each sold good or service. There were helpful neighbors and fresh fruit. The fruit was purchased from growers in upstate Connecticut or Massachusetts. The apples weren't preserved or waxed with added colorings to be more eye appealing. Real fresh fruit. Fruit that people chose to sell, and people chose to buy. I closed my eyes again.

I jolted awake this time as the chair tipped slightly over, brought back into this reality – this now – by a quick rush of adrenaline that allowed me to catch my balance and become aware of my surrounds immediately. The grandfather clock that was partially visible in the living room had ceased keeping correct time years ago and had settled on 2:42 with the exit of Aunt Josie from the cottage last year. I checked the dial of my Omega wristwatch, 9:30. I had been out for almost an hour. I took my cell phone out of its case, ignored the roaming warning, and dialed my wife Susan at home. She was just putting our son Alex down for the night, so I kept it brief.

Susan was a lovely, five foot nine, blonde hair, blue-eyed woman I had met in college. She drew me in with her Nordic features and perfect smile. We married in our senior year and nine months later, Alexander was born. He favors my side of the family in looks and temperament, despite the additions of Susan's strong jaw. He has the wavy brown hair and deep brown eyes of his Italian ancestors. As far as my son's name goes, there never really was a question about that. He has his great-grandfather's name that he shares with Nono-and with me.

Alexander Vincent Deluca. Another generation grew up farther from where we started, farther from this place of family roots. I put my cell phone on the table and inhaled the crisp night air.

I grabbed my briefcase and day bag, my lungs being satisfactorily refreshed, and walked through the living room to the wooden staircase. Both bedrooms were upstairs, and I remembered on cue which boards creaked and which would allow safe passage for a fifteen-year-old boy trying to sneak out for a night at the show or a bonfire on the beach. The theater had been replaced by a multiplex with adjoining bistros and a gelato stand for the affluent thirty-somethings that were trying to impress their twenty-something dates. But in my mind the one-screen theater and TasteeFreez needed to be experienced, needed to be lived and I had done both.

I paused for a moment at the bottom of the stairwell, running my fingers across the banister's oak. It probably didn't meet today's safety regulations, and the stairs themselves probably were not wide enough to meet today's code, but it was enough then. It was enough for the time when the eyes in the black and white pictures that adorned the walls were the colorful eyes of living, beautiful people. Fathers and mothers, uncles and aunts, cousins, and people we called "uncle "even though we were really never clear whether we were related or not. It did not matter. They were family.

And the family lived here. Walked here. Breathed this same air, looked at the same beach, admired the same pictures of weddings and confirmations.

Aunt Rose. Cousin Frankie. Sal. Noni. These pictures were taken in the prime of their lives. Or showed faces that were aging. Some I couldn't remember and that saddened me as I stood here. Their entire lives not written, not remembered, but somehow belonging to the cottage. They once had families and hopes, dreams and prayers. They laughed, they cried, they lived. And in this small cottage, a part of them remained.

I reached the top of the stair's landing and looked to the right. There I could still see Noni's bed. The lace coverlet fell gently over the sides, a small washbasin and pitcher resting as it had for years on a maple side table. I had found her here five years ago, smiling sweetly in her final repose. The Crucifix hung over her bed and a rosary in her small hand. Everything about her death said she knew it was her time to leave those of us who somehow tied our existence as a family to the strength of her character. The ones who had been shocked by her passing notwithstanding.

My grandfather, Nono, spent five years of his life working at a Connecticut Bus company as a mechanic to save up enough money to bring his new wife over from Italy. Uneducated and unable to speak the tongue of the new land, he, as thousands of immigrants did and still do, worked in manual labor practically around the clock to bring his bride – and their son he had never seen, to this land of opportunity and prosperity. It wasn't easy and at times it wasn't pleasant. But, in the end, my Noni's face told me that it had all been worth it.

I walked into the second bedroom, its thin blinds allowing the new moon to cast light shadows across the wooden floors. There were two twin beds in here and a small dresser separating them. I placed my briefcase and duffle on the closest bed, flipped on the light and let my eyes take in the surroundings. When had the easy chair been draped with a white sheet? Where was the playpen that had always been pressed up against the far corner closest to the south window? There was a water bowl on the dresser, but the pitcher must have been broken and thrown away in my absence. Thrown away. Was that what I was really here for? As estate executor that was my function, was it not? Sell off the cottage to the developer at an incredible price and split the money between the surviving members of the family. A bulldozer would reduce this floor to splinters and these walls to small blocks. And what about the memories? Where would the memories go as trucks filled with earthen remains ran trips to the closest landfill? The neighbors, for the most part, had already sold out and weren't they people like us? Didn't they have the same apprehensions that I had? Was their decision to sell any less traumatic or unsettling?

But it wasn't the neighbors who were selling now. It was my family. It was me. We, I -

was selling the hopes and dreams of four generations. This cradle of security, this most constant physical representation of our collective lives.

I looked down at my briefcase that held the final sales draft with a bit of disgust. As the only grandson, this task, just as funeral preparations, had also fallen to me. I received plenty of input of course, mostly from cousins and uncles that lived farthest away. It seemed the impetus to sell this man-made shrine grew with intensity as proximity decreased. Those who lived farthest away from its loving embrace were the most numb and apathetic.

4.

A copy of the family Bible (Catholic Edition of course) lay reverently by the covered chair on the small table whose green paint was beginning to chip off. The leather cover of the sacred book was worn from use, and it was heavy in my hand. Ignoring the bed sheet over the chair, I opened the Bible to its first page and began to read the entries of important events in my family's history. There was evidence of several hands in the past trying to come up with a family tree, recognizing the limits of paper and pen when confronted with such a daunting task. As the generations passed the names became more Anglo such as Vincent and Elizabeth becoming Casey and Chelsea, and then Micah and Brittany. Even in words, time moved on. But, like the cottage, the Bible still contained forever moments that did happen and needed to be kept alive:

Nov. 15, 1909 – Alex in America, New York City

Oct. 22, 1925 – Rose Carlucci marries Roman Annello

June 7, 1972 – Beloved son, Louis passes away

Feb. 1, 1982 – Florentine becomes citizen

The list went on for pages and pages. The Bible had more creased parchment in between Genesis and Exodus than the entire book of St. Matthew. Someone's hands wrote these entries, and these small sentences represented what life was to these people. My people. Me.

A small tin box that used to hold buttons was also on the nightstand, yet it now housed the Mass cards from funerals that had already begun to fade. Pictures of St. Anthony, St. Francis, and his prayer, Christ on the Cross and the Blessed Virgin reminded me of trading cards, the statistics on the back were the lives of the players. Some were written in Latin, recalling the ancientness of the card, when Masses weren't for the masses and the priests faced the altar instead of the congregation. "Nel nome del Padre e del Figlio e dello Spirito Santo, Amen," the words came back to me from some realm of my subconscious that still had a hold on the hours spent in Catechism and as an altar boy. Mass was a weekly affair. It was stoic and solemn. Men wore their best suits - most had only one - and women wore pill-box hats. Every little girl had on a dress with lace, and every little boy had been scrubbed thoroughly the night before. Sedans, all black, or the occasional blue, vied for the parking spaces that allowed the most unobstructed exit after Mass was over.

The bells would ring. Father Malone would enter after the Cross and Holy Book. At least two altar boys would follow Father as the ushers closed the large wooden sanctuary doors. These were the days before altar girls, before people started wearing jeans to Church, and genuflected, not bowed. The pews were hard and uncomfortable, and the Church- hot in the summer and cold in the winter. But we all came. You'd see three, sometimes four, generations of families sitting side by side, silently mumbling the mass to themselves in perfect time with Father Malone. And, aside from Holy Days of Obligation or special feasts and baptisms, Father Malone was done in exactly 54 minutes. You could set your watch by it.

After Mass, we'd push and shove our way towards Father, looking for that moment of connection when he'd recognize us in front of our parents. A quick compliment by a priest was a boon for the day as you could see mother's face blush with well-deserved pride. Her mother had felt the same way twenty years before, probably with Father Malone too, who I always thought had to be an eternal hundred years old. He was always gray, always wide with the lines of age, always respected and always marrying someone or, as the funeral cards in my hand reminded me, burying someone.

5.

At the bottom of the tin box was a single gold star, a present from the government in exchange for Uncle Gino's life in Vietnam. Noni had gotten a flag too, I remember, but she would rather have her son. Father Malone was there too, a beautiful service in front of an empty grave. I remember that it rained that day. It rained and the sky was dark.

I gently laid the Mass cards back in their proper place alongside the tin box. As I stood, I heard my bones creak slightly, another reminder of the time that passed unnoticed. The room was cool even before I unlatched the sill and shimmied the wooden window up its antique roller. I had always loved the smell of the salty night air, and this night was exceptional only in its larger scope. I wasn't here to enjoy the smells and sounds; I was here to sell them. I inhaled deeply. The cottage was the same. The beach was the same. The mist that gathered around the shore at this time of year every night was the same. But I was different- I was the catalyst, and my decision here would change forever a sanctuary, a way of life, a family's dream.

I needed sleep, and I knew it would come easily. I had flown four hours, driven the same amount and was now in the most comfortable and relaxing place I could ever imagine. I had in some way, this day, regressed to the comfort of generations of love, the familiarity of the surrounds nurturing my desire to belong and to be loved. I slid off my running shoes and unbuttoned my shirt. The bed was firm from the plywood that had always been placed between the box spring and mattress for support, and the down pillows were soft. Faintly I could hear the waves entering the cove as they had always entered, only to leave by the same route the next morning. I turned off the small light and closed my eyes. Sleep would come quickly indeed, I thought, as my mind let go of my conscious self and I became a part of the room, of the cottage, of this never-ending stream of familial memories.

A Chevy parked outside, and maybe a ride on Uncle Gino's motorcycle. Look at his tattoo! A Marine! Right out of high school and enlisted. A hero! "Let me ride."

"Throw it to me!"

"I can catch it Uncle Gino."

Flash of pearly white teeth against olive colored skin and jet-black wavy hair. Always a little stubble, even before it became fashionable. I think he started shaving at ten.

Board up - big storm. First one of the year. Let's get all the lawn chairs in. The picnic table won't go anywhere. Think the cellar will flood? We've got enough food here for an army. Can't be too prepared for a blizzard.

"Here, eat some bruschetta."

"Elizabeth - get your cousin something to drink. He's thirsty."

"Anyone want a sandwich?"

"Lori - get me some bread."

"We'll stay here tonight."

"Of course, we'll play cards..."

"Santiago, come down for dinner. Rosa is here." It was the school formal. Kodak bulbs popped; people smiled. Santiago almost fainted. Starched collar, mismatched socks, a pat on the back from grandfather and a punch in the arm from Uncle Gino. Saint Anthony's School Formal. A first date. A first kiss. Sneaking some altar wine before it had been blessed. Santiago and Rosa have three kids now: Sonny, Sandy, and Salvatore.

The evening grew cooler, and the night was still. There were no streetlights or neon signs touting 24-hour shopping mega centers here. Stars shown down gloriously from their exalted perch in the heavens, keeping watch over God's earth and this small cottage community. No dogs barked. No sirens blared. No noise from the freeway was to be heard. Branford was peaceful, tranquil, it was home.

6.

About 2:30 in the morning I awoke with a slight chill and walked downstairs. The screen was the only protection to entering the front door. I closed the wooden frame. I used the only bathroom, that was downstairs, and was briefly shocked at the coolness of the water flowing from the old copper pipes. Anyone who has never lived north of the Carolinas really has no appreciation for what really cold water is. The old pipes in nearly frozen earth produced the most refreshing temperature - somewhere right above freezing. I dried off my hands with a monogrammed towel that had begun to slightly fray. They were worn but added to the lived-in-feel of the cottage. This was a home that had always been alive - dynamic! Not a show home for unwelcome guests at an office party, not a static and sanitized house where children couldn't sit on the sofas or use the good China. This home had character and charm. Not every beam was measured or angled perfectly to a level, not every carpet fit the room without a little stretching near the baseboards. It was flawed as life is flawed, but that was part of its treasure.

I climbed back upstairs, left the windows open and put myself under the top sheet. The fluffy pillow had already adjusted to my head's form, and I could feel a slight breeze across my exposed chest. I closed my eyes again and sleep found in me a welcome partner.

SATURDAY

1.

As the morning sun crept over the eastern horizon and sent its rays rippling across the cove's calm water, sounds of seagulls and sandpipers drifted into a portion of my being that wasn't quite my conscious self but not quite a dream either. The small town was beginning to wake up to yet another beautiful day. The remaining fishermen that still trolled the mostly fished out coast sending friendly hellos to their friends and fellow fishermen. A few cars could be heard parking and unloading small children, the earlier the more likely to find a place to park where space was limited. Being Saturday, a few lawn mowers could be heard cranking up and running steadily and a few random shouts of joy from children being let out of the house after a long week of being confined to school. It was going to be a clear day, with just a little nip in the air - crisp but not cold.

The shore at this time of the morning didn't just look like poetry in form - it was. How many sonnets could be written about the mist as it had gently settled over the rocks of the peninsula's jetty? How many psalms could describe the light on the water and the effect it had on a person's soul? Was it impossible to imagine the great love stories being lived and spoken of in the crystal-clear shallow waters where young couples held hands for the first time as others remembered their own youth?

I had set no alarm, for this place and its surroundings did not lend themselves to such rigid constraints that man had crafted. Here it wasn't 2 p.m., it was sometime in the afternoon. Here people didn't get up at 7: 45, they got up with the sun. In winter, as the days grew shorter, the time asleep shorter too - perhaps the body's way of shouting, "I don't want to miss a minute of the daylight!" Here Easter wasn't a day, it was a season. Here fish wasn't for dinner, it was for

Friday. The grocer would get fresh fruit tomorrow, if not, most likely the next day. A different time frame existed here, a different set of rules to play by.

If one was sick, they would stay home. If dinner wasn't ready, you could snack on cold cuts or fresh fruit. Mass was the only time sensitive activity along the shore, and beautiful bells tolled to gather the flock. It was a place removed from decay. Yes, paint faded and needed to be reapplied, trees grew that had to be pruned and the salt air rusted anything metal from bike chains to watering cans. But something that really existed in its own time really couldn't decay; it couldn't leave that special place where it existed neither here nor there, today or tomorrow. This place was a constant. This place just was.

Somewhere in the distance, out of reach of this place, out of step with the melody of sounds here, I knew Susan was turning off an alarm clock and beginning the day's rituals with our son. They would be timed to perfection, right down to which turns to make to avoid hitting a red light at the corner of Boxwood and 7th. Breakfast was on the go, sandwich bags grabbed, car key dropped and picked up in one fluid motion, all with one object in mind: beat the clock. Save time. Well, here in this bed amongst the shrill gull cries and distant lawn mowers, the clock was beaten. Time and its passage were not allowed; the cottage kept its family safe. Each generation became the next generation seamlessly and predictably.

Yes, lives were being lived, and the small act of sitting up told me that my body was aging, but here, inside this sanctuary, that was OK. It was the way life had always been and the way it should always be. I opened my travel bag and stared at the contents as the fresh morning air brought me to full consciousness. I wasn't groggy or lethargic, I just needed a moment to process how different life actually was here on the shore.

I took a towel, a razor, and my toothbrush downstairs to the shower. Again, the familiar creaks and moans of the wooden stairs followed behind. Each lifted foot produced a unique sound that effortlessly blended in with the next before it disappeared. It was as if footprints in the sand that were quickly washed away by the tide could be set to music. It was an audible trail, a noisy shadow.

I had purposely not brought shaving cream with me because there was always a shaving cup with shaving soap in the bathroom's small medicine cabinet. It was my grandfather's old horsehair brush that I had always lathered with and gripping the well-worn handle was like shaking hands with an old friend. He had taught me to shave right here and although I have switched from his metal straight razor to a more accurate and reliable plastic import, the shaving cup itself was enough to trigger the memories again.

"Like this?"

"Yeah - if you want to cut yourself. Now watch. Always go up - careful! It's sharp. Keep the water cold. There you go Vincent. You're a big boy now. HA! Boy - a man! Look at you - you're going to have a moustache before your cousin Johnny and he's a year older!"

"Ow!"

"Santa Maria! Be careful. What's the matter for you - didn't you just hear what I said? Ha! It's good. Put some cold water on it. It's just a little nick."

I still have a tiny scar from the little nick I got here thirty years ago. But to be back in Nono's strong arms again and hear that hearty "Ha"! He was full of joy, so happy to be alive and here in Connecticut with his family in this cottage. Ha! Another clam. Ha! Another base hit in stickball. There was always something to be done. Ha! We need to paint the garage. Or something to be seen. Ha! Look at that bird's nest right up in my gutter. It wasn't an act or some intellectual understanding of the cosmos or how things worked in Washington - it was the joy of enjoying a simple pleasure without even being aware of it.

It was never ignorance - it was living life with a zest and zeal that now has to be taught at $500 per night conferences or bought on a series of tapes for three payments of just $39.99 each.

2.

I was only fifteen when we got the midnight call that Nono had died. I say only fifteen, because death had not touched my life up to that point. At fifteen it is a shock to discover that this life is temporary and that every moment somehow counts, and that every missed moment cannot be recaptured. My grandfather's absence left a void inside of me and inside of this cottage. It wasn't as loud anymore - he never seemed to talk at a normal tone, his normal tone being slightly less than a good-natured yell. That 'Ha!' of his passed from my life as he passed into the next and I found myself missing its reverberating effect on the highly polished wooden floors.

He had fallen from a tree that, at 75, he should not have been climbing. It was a project to trim back the oak tree whose enormous branches grew relentlessly over the porch of the cottage. He had fallen 30 feet from its top onto his back, his soul lingering with his body just long enough for his sons and daughters to come to his side to say good-bye. He was in pain, my mother told me later, and was really suffering, but he held on until the last of his children came to his bedside. Uncle

Sal who was living in Cleveland, then asked Father Malone to administer him Last Rites of the church. This final act of holding on until his family was with him - that was the strength of his character, personality, and his body's resolve. I could almost picture him lying there, looking at death. Ha! Not yet. You must wait for my family. Ha!

When I arrived with my father and two sisters the next day, my grandfather was already gone, and the lifeless form laid out in the living room of the cottage seemed not unlike a statue that could come alive at any time. Was he not just resting as he had always rested in the afternoon? Wouldn't he just get up and say, "Ha! Time to go back to trimming the tree?" I had run outside to the cursed tree, looking up into its violent branches, cursing it as Jesus had cursed the fig tree. I didn't want it to prosper. I wanted it cut down, torn up, and moved away from my sight. In my childish rage I swung at it, kicked at it, and called it every foul name I had ever heard. I did not know how it had changed my life, but I was acutely aware of the fact that it did. I did not know how it would be different here at the shore, I just knew that it would be.

As children ran in and out of the house and adults gathered around the coffin and tables filled with wine and cold cuts, I cursed the tree. Tears flowed freely down my face, the color of my cheeks turning red with rage and despair.

"Vincent!"

I turned around to see Bella coming toward me, and instinctively wiped my face.

"You okay?" Her small olive hands grabbing hold of mine.

"Yeah, Bella."

A smile. She stood next to me and looked at the tree. "I hit it yesterday too", my cousin said. Her smile dimmed slightly. "I miss him so much already. He was always so happy."

I had never talked about Nono in the past tense before. Just to hear him mentioned like that was unnerving and the tears came back to my eyes. "I'm sorry," I apologized.

Bella laughed and gave me a hug. "Let's go inside and leave this tree alone. Everyone's here and they'll want to see us. Well, they'll want to see you! You know how much competition I have? There are twenty-seven granddaughters and you!" Her blue eyes flashed brightly. "I'll just have to do something famous someday or no one will ever know I existed!"

"I know Bella - and I'll always know. I'm glad you came outside. I needed you."

"Hush, let's go find Noni."

And we walked inside together, hand in hand, each relying on the other at that moment of trial, learning what it meant to rest easily in the loving embrace of another. We would carry on the interdependencies of family - needing and being needed, caring for someone and being their friend. This is what families did. They got over things together. They grew stronger together. Nothing could break the bonds of family if one was willing to open their hearts and hold one another. It was the first death I remember vividly and the only time I ever kicked a tree.

3.

The shower was cold, even with the small hot handle turned all the way. Iced beads invigorated my body while stimulating thought as I reluctantly awoke. The shower stall was small in the cottage, no bathtub and only a curtain on an antique rod falling unceremoniously down to the floor. I used my soap as lather and shampoo and stood as long as my body would let me under the icy downpour. The water tasted great, and I quenched my thirst hurriedly from this indoor spring. No fog on the glass greeted me as I pulled the curtain back. At home in Florida, I took that for granted. Here it was different. Cold. As if people had been away far too long and their absence was present in every mundane task or activity.

I towel dried myself quickly, the gooseflesh already begging to grow on my arms and chest. My blood had gotten "thin" in Florida, too few winter days and too few cold showers. There was not enough room to fully dress in the small bathroom, even for a child. So, I hustled upstairs and threw on the same outfit I had worn since I was a teenager: blue jeans, t-shirt, and white running shoes. The brands had changed with age and success, but I felt the same here. The few gray hairs that were beginning to show in my deep black hair notwithstanding, I felt the excitement this place produced on every visit. The first day at the cottage! Up at dawn, a quick shower (in later years a shave) then slip on a pair of blue jeans and off for any adventure the day would bring. It didn't matter if the entire day was spent riding bikes, going downtown or simply milling about the shore with friends. Time wasn't our enemy back then, and the blind optimism of youth allowed our imaginations to soar and our desires to be innocent.

Summer vacations, winter breaks at Christmas and long weekends. Nothing compared to the first day at the shore. Adults would be sharing beds, children vying for the most comfortable sofa or the thickest sleeping bag. We were never alone here. There were at any given time at least ten or twelve of us descending upon this place, calling it home and making it a part of our lives. My sister Elizabeth playing with the younger girls Tina and Gina, Diane, and Rosa. Me, I'd always be with Bella and together we'd have the most wonderful of times. We both learned to swim here in the cove, and as teens made it out to the small barrier island just visible from shore. There was a house on the island back then, a retreat from reality for an elderly man and his only companion, a large German Shepherd. Swimming to the island and returning unscathed was almost a rite of passage to the teenagers at the shore, and Bella and I were no exception. We went out with the tide to cut down on strokes and swam with a fair amount of anxiety out to the island. Success! Bella and I touched land! Unfortunately, both man and dog had been watching us approach, and oaths were shouted at us along with a fair amount of barking. Bella and I became acutely aware of our predicament, and as we were too scared to run (and had nowhere to run to anyways), we jumped back in the water while evading several curses being flung in our general direction.

We eventually made it back to shore, of course, tired but exalted in our accomplishment, two best friends, rolling in the sand. Later that night I felt the leather of my father's belt, but Nono simply laughed and said, "Boys will be boys and Isabella will be Isabella! HA!"

I grabbed my wallet and headed outside. Out of habit I left the cottage doors unlocked and simply latched the porch's screen door. I decided to leave the SUV in the gravel driveway and walk the mile or so into what was actually quickly becoming a small downtown. The crisp air on my face was invigorating, and the calls of the gulls let my spirit soar along on a gentle breeze. The leaves on the oaks and maples had already started to turn color, reds and oranges dotting the ends of green leaves, reminding me that everything is temporal, and every life has a season. The leaves looked as if a child had dipped them haphazardly into fall-colored paint for a school project that wouldn't be finished for another month or so.

4.

The ground here was hard. Cold and hard. Despite the closeness to the shore, or perhaps because of it, the earth here was rough and strong, a perfect foundation to build a permanent structure on. I remember as a boy hearing stories of Nono and his sons digging out the cottage's cellar with only the simplest of tools and the brute strength of their backs – along with a fair amount of stubbornness of mind. It took an entire summer for them to accomplish this impressive feat, and Bella and I learned several Italian words that are quite unacceptable in most Italian circles that do not consist of men or sailors.

It was back-breaking work, the five of them - my grandfather, Cousin Leo, Uncle Gino, Uncle Sal, and my father. Only Uncle Sal is alive now, but the fact that these men existed and lived together - here - is proven by the monument to their determination and hard work for the family under the cottage.

They had gone down about five feet – I can't stand fully erect in the cellar – propping the cottage's foundation up with twelve-by-twelve beams Joey had acquired in some sort of trade the last time he was in New York. How he left with some chickens and wine and returned with treated lumber I'm still not sure about, but the beams are still as strong today as they were when the first one was successfully stood upright in the earthen cellar. The ground being so hard kept the cellar cool, and the firmness of the earth allowed for a natural set of walls. Racks for canning and a couple of wooden stools were eventually brought down after completion, and my grandfather ran a single electric cord downstairs with one 75-watt bulb. It hung evenly from the ceiling and allowed safe passage to and from the canning racks after the sun had disappeared over the western sky.

It was always cool with a slight feeling of dampness down in the cellar, and as we all got older the few steps down would have to be replaced. That was my first carpentry job – starting out as Uncles Gino's apprentice, then on my own after his death in the war. It felt good to add a little of myself to the cottage, knowing that to get in or to get out of the cellar one had to climb up or down stairs that I was responsible for constructing. This small act of building a few stairs or reinforcing an original beam somehow bound me in a permanent and tactile way to the laborers that had come before me, whose muscle and sweat dug the cellar that was now dependent upon me to maintain. It was a torch handed down in some way from generation to generation, a baton passed from one runner to the next.

With the birth of my son and Bella's two boys, there wasn't a question of whom I would eventually hand the old wooden toolbox to, but whether or not I would. The stairs could continue to be patched or replaced as needed – there were willing hands now, but if the cottage itself slipped away, would others find the need to? Would anyone ever remember if not the family?

I turned right at Limewood Avenue, small pieces of clay clinging to my new athletic shoes and began the mile long walk that overlooked the cove. The house on the island still stood, as did the ice cream parlor by the jetty. We used to fish for crabs and shrimp by night off the jetty's rocks, our kerosene lanterns bringing the tiny shellfish to the surface. A few years back I remember reading about a non-local boy drowning in the rip tide. His feet had apparently slipped off the jetty. It was almost impossible to drown or shrimp there now due to a fence that sectioned off the 'safe' side of the jetty. A resilient local could wade or swim around the fence and then climb the steep coast of the jetty and proceed to the end, but most just decided to do other things. This was a relief to the boy's family and the Branford shrimp population.

There were no sidewalks here along this one lane ocean view pass, but orange "x" marks and numbers written on the asphalt by surveyors told that construction was surely coming. The sea oats had already been removed back thirty feet from the road, and heavy equipment was being dropped off on parcels of land that had once been home to other cottages that had been home to the memories and stories of other families. Those cottages had already been torn down. Bricks and wood, shingles and concrete blocks had been trucked away to the dump near New Haven.

A car tooted its horn as it passed by, the driver waving a friendly hand, a bit of small-town kindness that only goes out of style when the small towns are no longer small. Then it won't be a toot, it will be a honk, and instead of a wave another less friendly gesture will be the good morning hail. But it was still a toot and a wave here, still a friendly smile and a nod of the head.

Across the street the beachgoers were unloading from trucks and SUVs the necessities required for creating a perfect day. Masks and rafts, coolers and cigarettes, portable radios, and TVs. The music and TVs were a recent addition, but the coolers were packed the way they had always been – apples and cookies, PB & J sandwiches, RC cola and maybe a couple of beers for Dad. I didn't see any fins for the kids – now they were wearing shoes that were made for walking on pebbly beaches, and the suntan lotion was clear instead of pasty white. Rafts and umbrellas were being rented at the ice cream parlor and a few hotdogs were already being sold. Blue cabanas dotted the beach, a day's rental going for twenty dollars – we used to pay three.

I rounded the bend and continued toward the center of town. The Carmichael's house still stood – it was a large, brooding wooden house, grand in the sense that it was three times bigger than any of the cottages. Jimmy Carmichael and his family were locals and had lived here year-round. We were roughly always the same height and weight even though I was two years older than he was. He owned the house now and his size seemed to grow in proportion to the rooms of the house. Although we were never close, he did marry one of my second cousins, so Susan and I still send them a box of fruit each Christmas.

Behind Jimmy Carmichael's house was a large pond that would host ice skaters of all ages every winter season. It was nestled in a clearing that was surrounded by a few pines and white birch trees. Lying on city property, it had recently been acquired by the same developer that wanted to buy our cottage. Jimmy Carmichael's boisterous posturing at City Council meetings had not been enough to keep the city members from voting unanimously to rezone the area commercial and approve its drainage.

In 1986 my cousin Tina had fallen through the ice and drowned there. It was the second time I had experienced death in the family but this time I didn't kick the ice or curse it. I simply cried. I knew somehow that I was maturing. I was a pallbearer for her funeral carrying the tiny coffin into the big church. Father Malone was there to give a solemn mass and lend a shoulder to a grieving family. She had been 5 years younger than me, my sister's age, and her death affected Elizabeth more closely. I've always wondered about families that must deal with the tragic loss of a child, especially now that I am a father.

I guess time just has a way of letting the past slip from memory - at least conscious memory. Uncle Sal and Aunt Mary went through some terrible times after Tina died, and her sister Gina was totally heartbroken. How do you tell a 12-year-old that her twin sister drowned? It was rough for the whole family. Red eyes and black dresses for weeks. A little spark went out of Uncle Sal's eyes. Something had permanently changed. You could barely notice it, but he was different. And time went on as months turned into years. He watched his darling Gina put on a white gown and marry Joey Feliciano and have kids of her own and the sparkle came back. By this time Uncle Sal had white hair around his ears and none on the top of his head but his laughter returned. He looked so proud of his grandchildren, more family to love.

I was approaching the intersection of Main and 1st, the downtown area of Branford. It was still early, (I had no idea of the exact time, of course) and the smell of fresh bread baking at Alonzo's scented the entire block. Alonzo Junior had taken over the business from his father in the mid-eighties, and a little Alonzo - who weighed in at a small three hundred - was baking today. He mostly sold to commercial accounts these days, but before the advent of superstores, lines would form every other day at Alonzo's at 8 a.m., noon, and 4 p.m. That's when we'd bike or run to town to pay a nickel, then later a quarter, for the piping hot Italian bread. We usually bought at least two - one to eat on the way home and one for the cottage.

Little Italy's Pizza shared a wall, and many customers with Alonzo's. Unfortunately, Luca had not been able to keep the business in the family because he had only girls that had gone off to college and gotten married. The food was still good and the new owners - a couple of Greeks from Pennsylvania - were smart enough to buy the recipes and hire local help, but I miss Luca yelling at the waitresses in Italian, and him cooking everything from memory. He had gone to live with one of his daughters in Toledo after he sold his place but came back to Branford a couple of years ago to fish and live in peace and quiet. His wife had died before I was born so it was now just Luca and a stray dog that he fed living above the restaurant he made into a staple of the community.

I saw the parking lot filled with cars from I didn't really know where. I turned the corner just north of the pizza shop. Looming before my eyes was a Big W where Branford grocery and the small Savings and Loan once stood. I crossed the asphalt sea and with a "whoosh" from the automatic sliding doors was instantly surrounded with bright lights and cold air, two things Branford Grocery never had. Elderly women were just starting to sample featured products on the main aisles. A lobster tank full of crustaceans, their claws neatly bound with blue or yellow tape. The loudspeaker called for a manager to come to aisle 25 to help a guest, and gentle music interspersed with product advertising completed the background noise of the supercenter.

It was an impressive store,don't get me wrong and the Savings and Loan had given way to a Wells Fargo office inside the grocery's giant walls. It just didn't seem like Branford. I missed the little wooden buckets that we'd carry down the ten grocery aisles. I missed the five or six wire shopping carts with wheels that were never quite balanced and the warped floor. The lights never seemed bright enough either, but Frank was always there, cutting meat and talking to his customers, and a couple of cute local girls would always be running the two cash registers. Almost every young boy that spent a summer in Branford would end up bussing tables at Luca's or bagging groceries for Frank. His brother, Michael, was in charge of produce and pricing. Each item was labeled with a small sticker showing the price, and each item had always been rung into the cash register by one of the girls. There were no shelf tags with bar codes or scanners at the register. A pound of meat weighed on a large white scale with a red dial. The dial always faced Frank - we just took his word that it was a pound.

The meat of course was never put into zip-lock bags or imprinted with a barcode. The meat was put on a piece of white butcher paper, folded by Frank in one fluid motion and held together with big piece of masking tape. The price would be scribbled on the package with a red crayon by Frank's flowing hand. Just the price, not what it was. You could tell by the smell when you opened it at home whether it was Provolone or Genoa.

The meat and the fish were always fresh. No prepackaged goods cured with sodium nitrate for freshness. Frank cut everything by hand on one of his two slicers. There was never a need for pulling a number and waiting to be called. Everyone waiting usually knew each other and would respect the other's place in line. Frank knew too, and would always call the next person by name..." Mrs.Bonezelli, the ham's good today...Miss Mary, how's your sister Antoinette? How about some fresh mozzarella Mr. DiVito?"

Frank was short and round and always wore the white apron that suggested his profession. His brother Michael that ran the fresh produce was the polar opposite. He was always in a shirt and tie, even in the summer, tall and thin, friendly but quiet. It had always amazed me that these two had sprung from the same womb.

I turned down the wine aisle to grab a liter of sangria when I heard Noni call from across the lawn and across the years. "Vincent! Isabella! Go up and pick me some dandy-lions!"

Dandelion wine. So up we'd go, Bella and me, to the open grounds near where this building now stands, the heat from the summer afternoon beating down on our necks, beautiful butterflies dancing in the air all around us.

The contrast in color was magnificent, and the outdoor spring smelled so very fragrant and aromatic. The rich green thin bladed grass that you only see in New England dotted with the bright yellow dandelion flowers against a bright blue sky with pearl white billowing clouds. Amidst this beautiful scene and causing it to flow gently through life as if in a breeze, were hundreds of brightly colored butterflies. The yellow and reds flitting by our two heads, oblivious to the fact that we were even there. Occasionally one would land on one of us, only for a moment, then – flit! away it went, searching for the perfect flower or the perfect mate. It was a background harmony to life's symphony played at full volume to all of our senses.

The hill smelled earthen and dew-like. We could hear Robin Redbreasts sing or an Oriole warble. The air was alive with motion, color, and sound, that left a pleasant feeling of completeness in our young bodies. Bella would carry the basket and I would pull off the prickly leaves of the dark green plants. We'd eat some later with oil and vinegar and a red onion. Noni would then use the rest to make dandelion wine with Uncle Leo, her brother. Even though we were only teens - just barely - we were always allowed to have a sip after the wine had sat long enough. It was crisp and bitter, and left a funny taste in our mouths, but the dandelion wine gave us bragging rights of semi-adulthood to my sister Elizabeth and Bella's sister Mary.

I selected an unpretentious bottle of sangria and added it to the soda and fruit in my basket. I bought some brie and crackers, along with a half-pound of provolone and capicola. Alonzo's hot bread and capicola had been lunch at the cottage for so long it felt natural to want it this day. On a boat fishing, a day at the shore, or just in from a stick ball game - there would always be cold cuts laid out on the kitchen table and a loaf or two of bread with a variety of cheeses. My grandfather would usually have some fresh tomatoes cut thick on a pull of bread (a pull means that I don't ever remember seeing a knife used to cut the bread-you'd just pull off the amount you wanted, and then the next person would do the same).

A selection of cheeses would include provolone, freshly made mozzarella, ricotta, and parmesan. Cheese was always white and the first orange cheese I saw just really didn't seem to be right. Bella laughed long and hard when I asked what this piece of orange square was on the Wonder bread at school. I think I was eight years old before I ever heard of American cheese and was in high school before I heard of Muenster. My ignorance in the culinary department was a source of great humor to her.

But that was Bella. Laughing, soft, gentle Bella. She was the baby that everyone used to stop and stay – "Wow! What a beautiful baby!" She became the young child with curly brown hair in pastel dresses that would make people stop and say "Wow! What a beautiful little girl! She's gonna break a lot of hearts someday." She became the focal point of desirability in high school, and I got into a fair share of fist fights over her protection to which she'd always hug me, give me a kiss on the cheek and tell me that I was the best cousin anyone could have. Then she'd flit off like one of butterflies on the hill. Her steps, a dance. Her shape and form, poetry. Bella was always carefree, living and growing into a beautiful woman. A few days later I'd be scuffling over what someone said about her again. And yes, as predicted, she broke a lot of hearts along the way.

I used my debit card to pay for my groceries, something that would have been as alien to the old Branford Grocery as the automatic produce water machines that sprayed a mist on the vegetables at predictable intervals. I chose paper, not plastic, more for nostalgic reasons than practicality and headed out of the climate-controlled superstore with a full bag. I walked back over to Alonzo's and although I didn't recognize any of the employees, I was so happy that this place still remained, despite the hundred or so varieties of bread offered at the Big W. The cooling racks and old brick oven were still the same, but the entire store had been remodeled with an up-to-date Seattle touch – small round tables and to-go bags emblazoned with a golden A on a forest green background. A rack behind the counter showed the new direction of Alonzo's to Branford's growing tourist population. Croissants and fresh bagels, muffins, and pastries. A cappuccino machine was worked by a young person whose gender was unclear.

The place smelled delicious though, and apparently Alonzo (or one of his offspring) had been able to make the transition from then to now, blending the taste of the past with the yearning of today's quick-paced society. I really wasn't sure if I should be happy or a little disappointed. I ordered my two loaves of hot Italian bread and only received a dollar in change from my five-dollar bill. It wasn't even enough to buy a cup of coffee as the forest green cups with the golden A were going for $1.50 each. But there were people here, laughing and talking about the latest news and latest happenings in the redevelopment plans for Branford. I could just barely make out some of the conversations of the sitting twenty somethings dressed for a casual day at the marina in deck shoes, white shorts, and Tommy shirts. I could hear distinct Boston accents, and English spoken in educated ways. A contrast to the memory of the local immigrants hollering their orders across a broken Formica counter to the original Alonzo, the one without the golden A on the forest green background.

I put one loaf in my Big W bag and pulled a piece from the second as soon as I left the bakery. Fancy new look or not, the bread was the same, the taste wonderful. The crisp outer crust ensured the soft inside exactly as it had always done, steam rising into the air, even on this warm day. I was tempted to stop at the small library that still stood on Second Street, but with my quart of milk and brie, along with the two mile walk ahead of me, I decided to wait and find out if they had "updated" it too. I had cringed when the library destroyed the card catalogue with the dewy decimal system after entering the information into a computer system that was connected to all of the other libraries throughout Connecticut and beyond. This had happened during my last visit here in the mid-nineties, and I was pretty sure any more updating would have been too great a shock to my already shocked system so early in the day. So instead of walking a block over, I pulled another piece of bread and began walking back to the cottage.

The distinct melody of Beethoven's Fifth alerted me to an incoming call. I put my package on the ground and tried to swallow the pull of bread I was chewing by the third ring. "Vincent," I answered as I flipped open the cover of my cell phone. "Good morning, Dr. Deluca, it's Tommy Fazio with Future Mortgage, I hope I didn't wake you."

I could almost feel Tommy drooling over the phone in anticipation of the commission he would receive when the cottage sold. "Not at all, Tommy", I replied, wishing I had bought a can of soda to wash down Alonzo's bread. Birch beer would taste just fine right about now.

"Anyway, Dr. Deluca, I was just calling to confirm our eleven o'clock tomorrow morning. I'll have all the necessary paperwork for the closing at that time."

"Of course you will, Tommy."

"I'm sorry, Dr. Deluca?"

"No, I apologize," I said, not wishing to be quite so flippant on such a beautiful day. "I'm sorry – I've just woken up and am feeling a little spunky that's all. Tomorrow at eleven will be just perfect."

Getting a little concerned about my milk, I decided to pick up the pace back out of town, past the Carmichael's house, past the drained pond, and back onto the beach strip of road. In my hour or so of absence, a foreman and a few day laborers had shown up to the recently cut asphalt, the majority of which seemed not to be doing anything in particular. I overheard a few comments about some of the young ladies sunning themselves across the street on the beach, and a few hints of cheap cigarettes could be smelled in passing.

5.

Connecticut was a union state, with union wages and union benefits. The unions were an asset to my grandfather in getting a job as a bus driver in New Haven. We were a union family up to Cousin Luca, when along with a guaranteed wage and set time off and overtime was exchanged for hard work and sweat. It was muscle not machine that had paved these roads and built the steel frames of the apartments in Hartford and New York. It was hard work, and you were glad to get it. Looking around at the orange-colored safety vests and hard hats standing idly about, I wondered what the general contractor was getting in return for his union pay. No one seemed to really be in charge, and no one really seemed to care.

I nodded my head at a few of the fellows that had sat down and wondered when the work on the road would actually occur. Was it all sporadic, a little here, a little there, or one big day of action that defined the project? A paradigm shift from incomplete to finished, from a generation of toilers to a generation of loafers. I crossed over to the beach side to watch the waves coming in as I finished the last mile of road before making the turn up the familiar gravel driveway.

I unhooked the screen door effortlessly and put the single bag of groceries on the wooden table. I put the milk and cheese in the refrigerator, and the wine and canned soup in the cupboard. I left the second loaf of Alonzo's bread on the table and poured myself a cup of ice-cold tap water that tasted as fresh and pure as my bottled spring water. Maybe I was hot and just plain thirsty from my walk and loaf of consumed bread. Maybe it was the red tin cup that Nono used to drink from; maybe it was just a frozen moment in reality, but for the first time since I had been approached by Future Mortgage's Tommy Fazio – I felt sad. A sense of sadness overcame my spirit – to me this house was more than just a house. Look, there on the stove, Noni's wooden spoon. Look at the stove itself – you had to light the pilot light and then turn on the gas burners. Didn't Uncle Sal and Cousin Luca drive two hours back home from New London just because they weren't sure they left the water running enough for the deep freeze that was expected?

What were these emotions? Were they brought on through tactile contact, a drift in memory, or a tangible entity that was the cottage and its memories? Was the place that held so much life, so much joy, not willing to be let go of? Did the tomato gardens want to be replanted, the cellar beams repaired, the couches filled with mothers holding their children on Christmas Eve after mass? Was there something about this place that somehow transcended wooden floors and concrete blocks? Is this what is meant by the difference between a house and a home?

Beethoven's Fifth. The caller ID showed it was Susan. I answered it on the second ring. "Hey, honey," I spoke almost inaudibly into the mouthpiece.

"Honey, hi! Are you okay? It sounds like a bad connection."

"No, I'm ok. I'm just standing here in front of the old gas stove. Do you know how cold the water is here?"

"I remember. Absolutely refreshing. I just dropped Antony off at my mother's and thought I'd call you. You sound down."

Smart girl. "Naw, just doing a lot of thinking."

"That's what you do best. Lots of memories springing up on you I bet. You've got a lot of your life invested in everything that happened there."

Very smart girl. "Yeah."

"Well, I love you. I've got to run. Do whatever you think is best for you and your family."

"Thanks honey. I love you a lot."

"Me too...oh, and Theresa called."

"Theresa?"

"Yeah, imagine. I think that's only the second time I've ever spoken to her. Talk to you later – love you."

Before Susan hung up, I got Theresa's phone number from her and told her that I'd call later tonight to talk to Antony. I stood silently looking at the ten-digit sequence of numbers. Theresa. And of all times, calling now.

Those of us who were third generation really never were told the story of what happened to Theresa or why she went away. She was five years older than Bella and me, and a decade older than my sister and the twins. She was in the older group of cousins: Monica, Collie, Valerie, and I only have spotted memories of us interacting as children or as young adults. The memories I had of her I always cherished. She was the smart one in the family, the first to graduate college, first to go to law school and always a beautiful smile on her face that was only eclipsed by Bella's. Theresa was someone you would naturally look up to. She was someone that was always going places, someone that was always going somewhere.

Then one day, she was gone.

Theresa had gone off to school determined to make the transition from blue collar to white collar. She had the intelligence to back up her quick wit and approach to ordinary situations. She was the one who could always linger on a point until the other person either saw it her way or was forced to give up. Many times, I witnessed different relatives throwing their hands up in frustration, turning red with anger and walking away from a heated debate with her. Even with my grandfather, Theresa held her own. He'd have given me a good smack had I not done what he wanted me to do right away – those being the days when parents and grandparents could actually use the rod instead of sparing it in fear of some intrusive neighbor watching. Heck, back then the neighbors were known to smack one of us boys in the back of the head or call our parents – then we'd really get it. Right across the back of our bottoms, twice if we really embarrassed our family. This translated into the school environment nicely, for the penguins (the nuns still had to wear the black and white habits then) were even quicker on the draw with the ruler than dad was with the belt.

But this is about Theresa. She that would be able to hold her own logically with anyone. Maybe that's where the rest of us went wrong, we didn't intellectualize everything, we were too busy being children. I don't think that Theresa was ever a child, or at least I never thought of her as one. She was always off by herself reading or listening to any debate she could find. She was in her glory during the Nixon debacle, when she was editor of the high school newspaper. Her writing was flawless, and her arguments were sound. It was frustrating. We all knew she would grow up to become a lawyer. Anyone that could tick off so many people and still not drive them away could be a politician or a lawyer. Since Theresa shunned the spotlight, a political career was never considered, even with the women's liberation push of the early 1970's.

The family was always kept abreast of her success at college, what awards she won and what clubs she had joined. Everyone was so very proud of her, and after her first semester at Chapel Hill, we all met at the cottage to welcome her home from her studies. She was to have two weeks off and then head back to North Carolina, where we were all sure she was both frustrating and impressing many a professor with her natural gifts and abilities. I was thirteen years old then, and Bella and Elizabeth were at the cottage with the twins, Gina and Tina.

Theresa's father, Victor, Uncle Sal, Nono and my father went to the Greyhound station to pick Theresa up early that morning. It was a good two hours' drive into Hartford and the family was anxious to see that young woman they were so proud of, so very proud. But she never showed up at the station. The ten o'clock train came and went, the one o'clock and Theresa wasn't to be found.

This being over thirty years ago, there was no cell phone on which to call her, no pager or email address. A computer couldn't produce a passenger list on demand and being late or not showing up wasn't a source of panic – things happened; people were delayed on occasion. So, the four weary travelers used a payphone to call the cottage and I told them Theresa had not called, and we had been inside all morning. Bella was instructed to make us all a lunch and wait inside until they arrived, just in case Theresa was trying to reach us. They were on their way back to Branford.

I always had a certain affinity for Cousin Theresa, not the intense affection that Bella and I have always shared, but more of a one-sided affection that a student has for a favorite teacher – I wanted to be like her. Vocal, rational, able to use her mind to get through situations that I needed to resort to my fists for. I wanted to study, become disciplined and be held with high esteem by all those in the extended family. I had the desire to achieve, but what I really wanted was to be favored, a common trait among children, I have grown to understand with the passage of time. What more could a child ask for than love and acceptance? If those at home continually praised your accomplishments and were pleased with your development, didn't that automatically transfer itself over into the world around in your personality, demeanor, and success? Conversely, a child that is stunted in development at home tends to meekly crawl into life, afraid of disappointing those around him or her, just as they perceived they had disappointed their family. Everyone wants to be the favorite, but only one can be. For our family – it had been Theresa.

My father was quiet when they arrived at the cottage. Noni making sure that Bella had fed the kids and Uncle Sal took a walk into town. I remember the look on Uncle Victor's face, not wanting to worry, telling himself there was a perfectly logical reason for Theresa missing the bus. But as when most tragedies occur, those closest to the hurt individual instinctively know – a gut feeling – that something just isn't right, regardless of if they can articulate their thoughts with proper words at that moment in time.

As the sun began to set and the sky went from blue to gray to black, a mood of oppression settled on Uncle Victor. Aunt Josie, Victor's wife and Theresa's mom had just pulled in from her job at Woolworth's in Hartford. Expecting to find her daughter in a home filled with laughter and cheer, food and fun, she instead found the kids upstairs and out of the way and her husband on the phone. He was trying to connect with someone in North Carolina that knew something about Theresa not being at the bus station. My father and Uncle Sal sat outside the cottage smoking cherry scented cigars and drinking anisette while

Noni was inside taking some oil and garlic chicken out of the broiler.

As the smoke drifted upwards to an open window, the five of us – Bella, Elizabeth, me and the twins, strained to hear any words that would make sense of the day's events.

"I'm sure she's ok…," said Noni.

"Yes, I know it's late, but I'm her father…"

"Doesn't look good…", my dad.

We didn't exactly know what 'it doesn't look good' meant, but the picture of a young girl traveling alone and outside at this time of night by herself was disturbing. This somber mood of the adults and the holding back of tears by Aunt Josie only reinforced the feeling we saw on Uncle Victor's face earlier. The feeling of being helpless and not knowing what to do about the fate of someone that you love. We didn't talk much that night – we listened, and sleep didn't come easy. Bella being a little older and more sensitive, seemed more upset than the rest of us, but as I have mentioned we never really knew what happened that day…only that it was something bad.

During the years, after Theresa had been found, there were whispers throughout the family from adult to adult, never allowing anything specific to be overheard by the children. There was something to do with a teacher and something terrible happening that night we had all waited for Theresa. We heard from her roommate that she had returned shaken and cold three days later, and Uncle Victor flew to Chapel Hill to retrieve the intellectual pride of our family. I didn't see Theresa at the cottage for about five years, although I had written several unanswered letters and sent many unreturned gifts to her new address, a private women's only college in upstate New York.

Her Chapel Hill roommate was perhaps the most accurate when she described Theresa as cold. It wasn't just body warmth, but something far deeper and more profound. When Bella and I finally saw her all those years later, it was as if a different soul inhabited the body we recognized to be our cousin's. In place of the strong-willed, assertive arguer, Theresa was now docile, reserved, quiet. It was as if a glass of water had been poured over the lit match that illuminated her hazel eyes. Cold. She didn't run to us when we flew down the cottage stairs to greet her. She stood off to the side, a shadow lingering in the shadows cast from Uncle Victor and Aunt Josie. Bella hugged her as was customary but received only a polite smile and "hey" in return. My greeting was even less well received. Theresa actually withdrawing from my advance for a moment, until after a reassuring glance from Aunt

Josie, she hesitantly allowed me to gently hug her small frame. I didn't know what had happened to her, but I knew I was sad.

6.

For the next thirty some years, as we all grew and aged, the unknown story of that terrible day could be assumed and needed to be left in the past. Theresa had moved on with her life in the best way she knew how, becoming a very successful lawyer in New York, defending the right of many injured souls. I say she was successful by the number of friends she had won over by using her time and good talent – mostly pro-bono – to be a defender of those that had no champion. Periodically, she would show up at a wedding or an anniversary party, but for the most part, it was her work that defined her role in life. The terrible tragedy that was to be her life's defining moment led to the help of hundreds of individuals – mostly women – that needed someone in their corner to fight for their right to survive as individuals, free from devastation by others. She had become a success; she had devoted a lifetime to helping others, but I still feel sad that her eyes never gained back their earlier inquisitive glare, and that of all the people she helped, no one had been able to truly help her.

But I kept trying. I would call and always talk to an answering machine or send a "thinking of you" card to her apartment shared with an oversized Persian cat, Atticus. I still sent flowers on her birthday and Christmas, but I never heard from her. Not a card. Not a call or note in the mail, in all the years. It's as though Theresa made it a point to excuse herself from my life and also that of the family's.

Until this phone call. Theresa had probably gotten my home number from Aunt Josie. After all these years and all of the grand adventures we did not share. Now, at this time, Theresa called. I dialed the number that Susan had rattled off to me and pressed the send key. One ring. Two. Three rings. Then a small, yet distinct, "Hello?".

It took me a moment to realize the significance of this call and that Theresa had broken down some wall, some barrier, for some reason and had called me. "Theresa?" I said calmly and with measured temperance.

"Hey." It was a soft voice, one that I would barely recognize as her own, or at least the voice I remembered as firm and controlling as a child.

"Are you ok?" I asked, fully cognizant of the words I was saying and the tone that was being used. I neither wanted to talk down to her nor unnecessarily put her in an uneasy situation by sounding too inquisitive or too verbose. I knew it was a verbal tight rope I was walking on, and yet my heart just wanted to cry out – "I've missed you! Let's be kids again! Let me once more learn from you! I've grown and done many things and I want to share them with you. Please let me!" Instead, after asking if she was ok, I backtracked momentarily and stammered, "I mean, are you doing well...is everything going good?" I realized I was tripping over my own words, and that I could fall at any minute, but I just needed to keep her on the line, needed to hear her shallow breathing, needed to feel the familiarity of an old friend.

"Yeah, I'm ok", from the other end. "I'm still in New York, you know."

A pause followed in which I was tempted to jump in and ask a thousand unasked questions, a hundred needed answers. Why weren't you here? Why have you let yourself be taken from the warm embrace of our family? You would not be judged by us, only welcomed with the open arms of people that have always loved you just because you are part of our family. But I didn't say any of that. I knew the time wasn't at hand. Perhaps one day there would be a natural exchange of ideas, a real honest-to-goodness talk, a welcome exchange by two people that still needed each other. But this was not the time. This was a beginning. This was not a cry for help or someone asking for a favor. This was someone calling for a specific reason, wanting to say something and not necessarily hear anything. But it was a start, I felt, and that was worth it. "The weather ok up there?" I asked.

"Kind of crisp.... Listen, Vincent, I need to ask you a favor."

"Sure...anything," a bit too quickly, a bit too needing. A pause followed.

"Yeah, ok. I was thinking about the cottage and everything and everybody…. you know, how we used to go to the shore as kids. I know you are executor, and I really haven't been a part of your life for quite some time now and I really don't have a say in the matter – I haven't earned it, but…"

The words were flowing quickly, and all made sense, but the words weren't the coherent case – logical statements of a respected attorney. I recognized the words from a child. Perhaps more of a child than Theresa had been when she was a child. This wasn't a debate or a reasoned thesis, this was a plea from someone trying to hold onto something that they were sure had already slipped away somehow.

"Go ahead," I said with compassion and conviction.

"Well, I just think it would be a shame if the cottage was sold off. I know that some of the family thinks a little extra money would be great around the holidays and all, but I think it's more than just a cottage, isn't it? Isn't it more to you?"

The question hung in the air for a moment while I tried to make my emotions, my reasons, and my joy at hearing from Theresa, somehow mesh together.

"You know I still have the key," she said, after realizing I was unable to articulate any response to her question. "I've kept it all these years, but I hadn't gone back until last year."

This was more conversation from Theresa than I had in thirty years of trying to engage her in some sort of familial relationship, and I realized that I did not want the sound of her voice to stop. I let her continue.

"Last year when I went back I kind of understood. I didn't know if it was just some form of nostalgia or if the pictures on the wall reminded me of a simpler time, a time I forgot about. But it was a good time. I stayed there for a week and walked along the shore a lot, read things other than legal briefs, and just enjoyed myself. That's when I realized that this is about what the cottage has always been. It's like a safe haven for old memories and a petri dish to grow new memories in. I still talk about that week I spent there. Those memories that I'll have the rest of my life. I'm not quite sure that I want the catalyst removed."

Now she was beginning to sound like the Theresa I had once known. The cottage wasn't just a cottage, it was a catalyst for events. I smiled at the thought of a young Theresa using the same rationale to convince Aunt Josie she was old enough to drive the Ford. "It just makes sense. The time I save driving to and from school as opposed to taking the bus could be best applied to more study or a job. I'd have the freedom to not rely on a faulty bus system that shuffles people though a system like herded cattle, none willing to demand anything more than they got." It had been logic and reason, compare and contrast. It did my heart good to hear Theresa talking like that once again.

"So anyway," she continued, "I found out from Sophia that the family had decided to sell and that you had been chosen to represent the estate. I've had my hand in a few cases that have involved property and they've all resulted in momentary happiness with long-term questionable pleasure. A bit of money may tie in nicely for the holiday, but in the long run, it's my experience that the sellers usually regret parceling off land and homes, unless they have been purchased for investment purposes in the first place. We all know how our grandfather never wanted the cottage to leave the family. If he was alive today, he'd still be living there, cooking noodles or fish and growing his tomatoes in that little garden of his."

My cell phone beeped with an incoming call that I intentionally ignored, needing to hear my cousin's voice and listen to her reasons.

"There were a terrific number of good times at that cottage, Vincent."

"There were."

"We were a part of something unique. Most families have nothing like this. I don't think most people nowadays do…and I think they miss out. I think I've missed out. I've missed out on so much, but in the back of my mind I've known the cottage and the family have always been there. I could go back. That time did exist and all I have had to do to recapture it was to open a door and walk inside. The cottage is like the family personified. It represents what warmth and comfort can be found at any time, without any pretense."

I spoke painfully direct. "Theresa, we all feel this way, but we haven't been back because we never left. This is hard for me, too, and I wish my father was still alive to handle this for me. It wasn't something unique that happened when you stayed away. We all started to stay away. We moved out, had families, shared holidays between two sides. Each time we would come back, fewer of us would be here. I love this place with all my heart, but I can't for the life of me get my own son excited about staying here for a weekend, let alone the whole summer. He hardly knows his cousins – some he hasn't even met. We've got family spread throughout the United Sates, and every single one can give you five excuses for not staying up here at the beach. There's never enough time. Can't get off work. Got to kennel the animals. There is always a reason to stay away –

when we were kids it was just a given that we'd always be here, that this cottage would keep everyone together. But people move away. I hate doing this – I haven't even been here in years. But I was the one who stayed."

"I just wanted to tell you that I always liked the thought of the cottage being there, even if I was not." Theresa said.

She was breaking my heart.

"Yeah. So, are you and Joe doing ok?"

"Yeah. I just thought I should tell you. I'm sorry that I bothered you, Vincent."

"No, no, Theresa. It's not a bother! I'm excited that you called and I..."

"Ok. I've really got to go. Take care." She hung up. Thirty years, and she was still running, still trying to belong, and letting people in just enough and no more. Thirty years later a phone call. Thirty years later she was still breaking my heart.

I sat down on the small wooden bench, the implications of this call entering my consciousness. This was something of worth, something of value, something to be treasured. Even Theresa found the cottage a place of refuge, a place so important that a thirty-year self-imposed verbal exile was worth breaking. She had called me, and I felt at once special and aware of my role here. In her eyes it was me who was turning the few fond memories she had of a too short youth into a barren wasteland. I was the physical manifestation of the demise of her past. I was contacted not out of the sense of love and camaraderie I had yearned for all these years, but out of a sense of fear. The fear of losing something precious. And again, it was Theresa that was losing.

But wait! That wasn't fair! I was losing too! I didn't ask for this responsibility. I assumed it in place of my father. This was what he was supposed to do, to make the decisions that affected the family, not me. He was named Vincent too, and sixty years wasn't enough. He should be here right now, taking care of this mess, bringing the family back together and making the tough calls. I had enough responsibility to my own family – my son was in school, Susan wanted another baby, my patients needed me. What an example I would be to them now – blaming my dead father for a phone call that bothered me from an estranged cousin. I could see myself writing the prescriptions already and doling out the advice that had almost become cliché in my field of psychiatry during my career. You have some unresolved issues with your parental figure. Your longing for your cousin is a manifestation of the need to fill a void in your own intellectual life. You are fifty and realizing that you must fully assume the mantle of responsibility, especially within the confines of a patriarchal family structure. Here's a prescription for Xanax, once a day, and I'll see you in two weeks. Make sure you talk to the receptionist on the way out.

7.

Yeah, I knew all the answers all right, and even most of the questions. I would intellectualize myself silly here at the beach, each person's life a portion of a great masterpiece, a relief that was alive. I would make myself understood intellectually just fine, and financially some of the family would benefit from the sale of the cottage. Aunt Josie had been ill lately, and Uncle Sal's meager retirement package had been stretched pretty thin of late – but I could not come to terms with this place on a level of experience I had never known existed.

I had counseled many people who had been struck with the notion that there was a certain 'feel' or 'soul' to a place, an attachment to an old house or special event that stood as an exceptionally extraordinary moment in their life. Some were good, some were bad, and although I understood their words, it was becoming quite clear that I was not identifying with them from a personal perspective. Until now. This place. This home. These memories. It was all of life and more, encompassing generations of experiences all wound up together in one big messy ball. That's it, I guess. Our lives were like a big pot of spaghetti noodles. Very intellectual, doctor. I poured myself a glass of red wine. Somewhere it must have been 5 o'clock, here it was only noon.

I decided to sit in Noni's parlor while I sipped the red vino, her little serving room where an unfinished afghan lay draped over a small rack waiting for hands that had long ago grown cold. Crocheting was another one of those lost arts that Wal-Mart deals and time constraints had all but eliminated. Needlework, sewing, crocheting – no one seemed to be learning the traditional pastimes in an era when everything was cheaper to replace than fix. Noni had sat here in this small rocker for God knows how many hours, patching skirts, hemming pants, mending Nono's trousers. Trousers – another archaic word that fit in better with the generation that addressed packages to young men using the prefix 'Master'.

When I was 'Master' Vincent Deluca I remember quite clearly and with much fondness the year we – meaning all twenty-seven cousins – all received afghans for Christmas presents. How many years had Noni worked on these woolen blankets? How many hooks and latches did she have to complete to pass on these labors of love? And each afghan was unique. Mine was a dark forest green. Elizabeth's was yellow and white, and Bella's was a combination of pink and red. They never really got that much practical use at home, my mother and father keeping them on the bed as a decorative cover in the seventies, when for some strange reason, everything in the house needed covering. The lamps had shade covers and the couches were under huge throws. I was happy when the fashion of the seventies passed (until it resurfaced like a badly dressed phoenix rising from the ashes in the late nineties), but I still have my afghan.

Tiny hands sewing sweetly to the beat of Tommy Dorsey or the crooning of Ol' Blue Eyes. The needle rhythmically keeping time with its up and down continuous flow. A tiny flash of silver was the thimble, reaching for a straight pin on a pin cushion that looked like a tomato. Yes, this was a functional sitting room, a room that had produced durable goods, goods that would continue in the family and produce memories. Tiny hands wielding tiny tools of the trade; thread, needles, crochet rods. It was all done out of love, all done willingly, all done without a second thought, and all taken so very lightly. Just a quick "thanks" and then off to do other things. A thank you card for a birthday sweater when I wanted a stickball and Bella wanted a pony for one of her dolls. But this room still held the patterns like a bank holds its vaulted treasures. Each stitch was firmly kept record of here, each shirt that was mended was remembered.

A small water ring was permanently set in the wooden side table where Noni would rest her coffee. The pillow that was on the chair was perfectly positioned to her back's comfort, and a few pattern magazines were in a wooden basket that my grandfather had made by hand for just that purpose. Neither one of them ever wasted much time on things that were not practical. If there was a need, it was taken care of. If Noni needed a basket for her patterns, her husband fashioned one in his workroom. If Uncle Sal needed a patch on his bus trousers, Noni would press one on. The gifts were practical – the sweaters and blankets, the shoehorns, and the boot removers. The boot removers! How funny. I remember when I was eighteen or nineteen getting a V-shaped block of wood that was angled so one end was off the floor about three inches. I had no idea what it was. It was Nono's invention that still must be in an attic of mine somewhere- I know that I would never throw that away. You simply put one foot on one side of the board and your heel of the other foot in the center of the "V" and lift...your boots or shoes would come off without having to stoop down to pull them off, or without ruining the backing by stepping on the heel with your other shoe. It was practical and ridiculous at the same time-but it was something from love, and something from the practical-thinking mind of the generation that lived through the great depression years. A block of wood, a few nails, and time. A simple and thoughtful gift that provided a use for a specific task. It's got to be in the attic somewhere. I made a mental note to check for it when I returned home and took another sip of wine.

8.

Noni's pillow was a little low for my personal comfort, but I didn't adjust it. I wanted it to remain how she had left it, in a perfect position for her small body, waiting for her to return, to pick up the needle and begin making something practical for Christmas time again. I sipped my wine and closed my eyes. Outside I could hear the last of the robins sing before they began their thousand-mile trek down the east coast. The day was cool, and I had opened the window of the sitting room inhaling the shore's salty mist. I began to realize how much the cottage not only meant to me but embodied me. Everything here was a memory. My memories were here, and it was here that I felt most alive. No matter how many years had passed since I had stayed at the shore, through the moving, marriage and children – this place was a constant. A constant for me, and apparently for Theresa also. This place was in my blood, it engulfed me with the feeling of warmth and belonging and ran through me manifesting itself in my actions.

How many times had I felt drawn here through a behavior or action that I had learned in this place? That Ha! of Nono's or the afghans of Noni's. I learned to swing a hammer here, learned to swim just across the street in the sound. I ice skated; had my first crush and later, kiss here. My father taught me how to drive down the narrow gravel side streets. My mother showed me how to form gnocchi and make stracciatella- the Italian wedding soup. My first tie was tied in the living room, a huge Windsor knot for my first day of Catholic school. The values and the life lessons were both clandestine and overt. A simple command to mow the front yard taught responsibility and a swift slap on the backside taught me there were limits and lines that I could not cross without repercussion. I had learned to listen to my elders, hold the door for ladies and remember to say please and thank you. These were all behaviors I would use all my life and later, teach my own son.

For all of the cottage's lack of amenities- one bathroom, no tub, never a microwave – it held an identity, and I began to realize that the identity it held was my own. Now that I was here, I began to realize that my quest in life for success – a home, a family – was a quest to what was already in existence here. All of my trials and tribulations, the late nights studying, and the proper raising of my son all reflected an innate desire to recreate this atmosphere. Even my desperate attempt to rekindle a relationship with Theresa could fit into this mold. I wanted not only to be like Nono, I wanted to be Nono. I wanted to have the calm security of love that was in this place. I wanted to have the trust of my son that Nono had from his. I wanted my Antony to be the well-loved everyman Uncle Sal was. I wanted to recreate this world with different players, escaping back to a time of comfort and simplicity. That is what my heart yearned for, that is what was the desire of my soul.

Every so often throughout my adult life those feelings would resurface. I would find myself longing for this special place. Usually, it was after a hectic day, or a certain sound – like the closing of a screen door, or a certain smell – like a cedar chest, would enter into my everyday life's routine. I'd smile, wish for a moment, or even daydream a little about how to make the idea of recreating this place feasible, and then go on my way. But here and now, totally engrossed in familiar sights, tastes, and sounds, wrapped securely in the arms of a benevolent memory, I inherently knew that I did not want to recreate this- I actually wanted what was here. I believed I dozed off for a few moments and the further I drifted into unconsciousness the more introspective I became.

"I can't wait to graduate this year," me to Bella.

"I'll bet. Even Theresa didn't score as highly as you did on the ACT. I'm so very proud of you!". We hugged. "I wish I could have been able to go off to school."

"You'll do just fine, Bella. Really. So, you have to stay a year at home, but next year you can go to a junior college." I knew that she wouldn't though. Even then, with so many suitors at a young age, Bella would be married with a baby or two before I got my bachelor's degree.

A pleasant smile came across her face. "I'll really miss you, Vincent. You know, I can come up to visit you on the weekends and we can plan to spend time together during your breaks."

"I'd like that. I'll make a lot of people jealous," and I knew that to be true.

That beautiful white smile and a faint blush across her delicate face. "Will you be leaving right away?"

"That's the plan. UCONN is only half a day's drive from here. I'll be able to come back if dad and mom need me, and they'll be able to come up if they start missing me too much. It's the perfect distance. They need to plan to visit me, they can't drive that far and me not be there, so they'll have to call first."

We were walking, as we always did, hand in hand, by the small pond. We had both just turned eighteen, and I'd be leaving for the University of

Connecticut within the month. Bella pulled herself close to me and rested her head on my shoulder. It was so comforting and wonderful. The scent of the evergreens behind the Carmichael place lingered and the sun shone perfectly against a pale blue sky. There seemed at that moment to be a limitless set of possibilities ahead of us. We could do anything, go anywhere. We were still so very young and the bond we shared was almost tangible, almost an entity in itself.

The path by the lake led around to a small jetty after crossing the two-lane road. We were still hand in hand, conscious of nothing else but the boundless possibilities of youth with a best friend that understood you completely. There was no need for words, and they were few and far between. A wisp of Bella's dark brown hair fell over her eyes in the gentle breeze that came from the shore, her face becoming moist from the mist that filled the breeze with small drops of salt water. Her skin was tan, and her blouse billowed over her small frame. I had never been more at ease in my life, feelings of hope and dreams as yet unrealized in my heart as well as my mind. Nothing existed anywhere else in the universe at that time for me. Nothing needed to. This simple walk with Bella was all of existence and all of the possibilities that were ahead of us were simply dots on the horizon. This was worth living for.

We sat on the jetty together, oblivious to all who were around us, even if anybody was, occupying the sum total of each other's existence. We were two of us, but we were also one. We watched the water come in slowly, and just as slowly leave the cove. There was no immediacy in anything. The sun barely moved, and the water's motion was almost imperceptible. We were both having the time of our lives, talking about the future, remembering the past, holding on to each other. It was in that moment of perfect serenity and beauty, repose, and awe that Bella turned her head toward mine, found my eyes with hers and kissed me lightly on my cheek. We smiled and sat silently together.

9.

At her wedding three years later, she was radiant. Both men and women stopped to stare at the beauty of the young bride. Bella was marrying Jimmy, the most successful of the many suitors. He was ten years older than she was and had already been down the aisle before, but he was disarmingly charming, handsome, and from a very well-to-do family. While the marriage only lasted two long years, Bella was to have a son, my nephew Alex, who favored his father's masculine build and his mother's picturesque features.

She was beautifully dressed in white, and I was proud to stand up for the new couple. The party lasted all night, dozens of family members, and well-wishers from both sides in constant motion throughout the rented hall after a beautifully scripted mass. I dreamed of her smile and how wonderful she looked, so young and fair, having been a part of my family, my life, for so many years. Now she was going to be part of another life....

I stretched on the small chair and woke myself. The dreams had been pleasant, and I sat debating whether or not to wake myself fully or try and recapture the moment I awoke from. I smiled. Yes. These dreams were all part of this experience of life. Bella, Jimmy, Alex – later more children would be born. But Bella was still there, in my heart, like this cottage, a living breathing portion of my life that I could never let slip away. I would fight for this relationship – but never needed to. The single most defining reason for this was simple. Out of all the people that had come in and out of my life, whether family or friend, acquaintance or lover, Bella had always been constant. She had never let me down. Every person, from my father to my sister – even Nono, had, with or without realizing it, failed me in some way. Maybe it was a harsh word said in haste, or a promise unfulfilled, but every person had a flaw. Except Bella. She was unique and even with the incredible amount of time we had spent together, years of understanding and closeness, there had never been anything except love and trust. Bella had always been there for me, always known just how close to get and when, and had always stood by my side. Even Susan, as wonderful and magnanimous of a woman, had her moments. Sometimes, as in any relationship, there were moments of despair or bursts of anger.

Anyone over the age of fifteen could probably count the number of close friends on one hand, but a person that never let you down? Someone you had shared every intimate moment with, talked in depth for hours to – could one really expect another person to accept you for who you really were, without losing respect - even after the dirty laundry had been aired? This was unique, Bella and me, and I was glad for the beautiful images of her happiness created by my slight dozing off. Bella always brought a smile to my face, and I wished she was here with me now, a smile on her face, a warm embrace, a kind word.

She had never moved more than twenty minutes from Branford and was with Michael now, a kind and compassionate dentist who had a way with Alex that his own father never had. I respected Michael and his love for my cousin and envied the love that he received. His love for Bella shone through his every action, doting on her as one would a favorite child, showering her with gifts of love and affection, both tangible and from the heart.

My life with Susan had not been quite so fortunate. We had our good days and our bad, and when it was good it was really good. And when it was bad, well, it was bad. I hadn't known Susan for more than a month when we decided to seek out a Justice of the Peace and have a quick ceremony with a couple of friends. That set the tone for the whole family, of course, no big Catholic wedding, or hundreds of guests, no planning, and no one other than Bella and my sister Elizabeth had even met Susan. We had been going to the same university and met in class during our senior year. I was only twenty-two then, and she was twenty-three. We had rented a small efficiency in Coventry over a local tailor's shop and continued our courses together. Susan was at college to find a husband, and apparently a passionate Italian with strong family roots on the fast track to becoming a psychiatrist fit the bill pretty well.

I'm not complaining – our marriage has lasted two decades, far longer than most people of my generation, but it hasn't been all roses. I wanted children from the get-go, she wanted to wait until I was established in my own practice, so we compromised and waited. She's very loving and true to me and I'd be hard pressed if it came right down to it to find someone that would have stuck by me this long. I know I have a fair amount of idiosyncrasies and can be pretty demanding of myself and others. We like the same movies, have mostly the same friends, and enjoy several hobbies together. Little Antony came along in an effort to add some extra passion and love to our relationship, a few years after the usual seven-year itch. She's really been a great mother to Antony and slowly but surely has won over my family with her quick wit and social graces, but I guess what I really feel I am lacking sometimes is that special connection that I have with Bella and can see in her relationship with Michael.

There seems to be a special wordless acceptance that some people are fortunate enough to find in another person and I'm old enough with enough water under my bridge to realize that it doesn't happen all too often. It's a feeling more than something concrete, something that transcends time and situation, and is always present in word and deed. A conversation that can be picked up weeks later, a simple glance that opens the soul's window, a smile that comforts. It could be hours of talking on end, or hours of sitting in silence in one another's presence. Both are time well spent but lead to a greater understanding of the other person and add depth and breadth to the relationship. That is what I had longed for with Susan, but in practice knew I could only have with Bella.

10.

I looked up at the small grandfather clock whose pendulums were motionless in the living room that joined the place where I sat. The dial was fixed on nine twenty-seven and had probably been that way for ten years. I glanced at my Omega watch; it was almost one-thirty. With a few creaks and cracks and an almost inaudible groan that accompanies standing for anyone that has hit middle-age, I got up from Noni's old rocker and decided to do a quick cleanup of the cottage. The deal with Tommy Fazio wasn't dependent upon the cleanliness of the cottage, it was the land that he was brokering a deal for, but somehow it felt almost disrespectful to be here and have the cottage not be clean. It was always lived in, but it was always clean. Looking around at the collecting dust and settling stick from the ocean's spray, I began to feel bothered for some reason, and I walked outside onto the screened-in porch Uncle Sal had made to retrieve a bucket and rags that I knew would be there, because they always were.

From outside on the front porch, I had a perfect view of the shore, by this time already filled with hearty beachgoers that weren't' about to let crisp temperatures and a little roadwork dampen their spirits on a bright day with blue skies. Only a few had entered the water, the temperatures already too cold for anyone other than locals or maybe a visitor from further north. The sounds of gulls could be plainly heard, yet their cries were far less dense than when shrimping off the jetty was still allowed, and small dinghies would lead seasoned fishermen to their traps or larger boats anchored just within the cove's deepest waters. A few children would feed sandwich crusts to the gulls, until a frustrated mother or father would become annoyed enough at the hovering birds and tell their children to stop. Round and round the gulls would fly, some landing occasionally to investigate the remains of a crab that had washed in with the tide or to perch momentarily on one of the roped off pier pylons. The sandpipers searching for lunch ran back and forth from the water's edge, avoiding getting their feet wet as well as the path of seniors that walked constantly on the hard-packed sand. Both the sandpipers and the seniors seemed wary of the water, both looking for something and being instinctively drawn to the life-giving shore. The sandpipers usually found what they were looking for, but I cannot speak for the seniors, yet every day they came.

My first task of cleaning was removing the cobwebs and dust that had collected in the corners of the porch; a broom and a small two-step ladder was all I needed to begin this task. I was in no particular rush and enjoyed being alone with my thoughts and the sound of the gulls. The porch was shaded now, the tree that had taken my grandfather's life had not lost its leaves yet and the distinct smell of fresh baked pies drifted in on a faint breeze. There were only a handful of cottages that had not been acquired for redevelopment by this time, and of the few that still remained, only three still had full-time occupants. The pies were coming from the Donovan house, alerting me that a visit from one of old Mrs. Donovan's grandchildren was forthcoming.

Old Mrs. Donovan had been old ever since I was very young, and I could remember playing stickball with her grandchildren years ago. She was one of those perpetually older people-those that seem to have aged from their first appearance in your life and every time thereafter. It felt to me that she must be in her nineties by now, still holding onto her independence, still holding onto her cottage, still baking her pies. I had never met her husband and have never heard anyone speak of him. To me, she had always seemed like the perfect American grandmother, a bit out of place in the small Italian enclave here at the shore. She wore ironed aprons when cleaning or baking, baked pies instead of cakes or cannoli, planted flowers instead of a garden and didn't wear black every day to show her perpetual state of mourning for the husband I assumed she once had. Her house wasn't as lived in as ours was, and despite the constant stream of relatives in and out of her cottage, one got the feeling that the visits were all planned. Mrs. Donovan didn't give the aura of one you just dropped in on, like Noni or any of my aunts. We just showed up here at the beach. It was just a part of life that was taken for granted. Mrs. Donovan's children called first, made plans to visit and already knew how long they were staying. Visiting for the Donovans was just that – visiting. Their lives were separate and intersected with hers for a period of time, but then the children and grandchildren would say goodbye and plan to come back. We just came back.

She did bake good pies though and after a bit, the Donovans were treated less as an oddity and more as an eccentricity. Her Christmas tree was never real like ours; it was silver and came in a box. Meals were held at regular times every day, not just eating throughout the day as we did, snacking on yesterday's sausage and stuffed shells. They didn't go to mass either, they went to church, and I remember one time being surprised that their family Bible didn't have as many books in it as ours did. But they were social, and you could find one of us over at the Donovan's cottage almost every day when the kids were in town, the boys swapping stories or playing ball, the girls playing house or having tea parties. And she was still here, baking pies for the grandchildren – baking pies all these years later. They smelled delicious.

I had it in my mind to go ahead and scrub down the floor on the porch, so I began the task of moving the small boxes and tables that had accumulated outside to be sorted out. The porch, like the tiny attic, had become a catch-all for storing things that we knew we'd never use but could not part with just in case. Weathered boxes of childhood games, old pots and pans, plastic doodads, and a bag full of garbage bag ties made up small piles of keepsakes that I stacked on the front lawn. I pulled a trashcan over from the side of the house, disturbing a daddy long legs spider that had made its home between the wall and the can's metal lid. Many pincher bugs and a couple of earthworms dug deeper into the soil as the can exposed their dark lair to the sunlight, the damp dirt eventually drying throughout the day.

Most of the items on the porch went straight to the garbage can, there really didn't seem like any good reason to hang onto the bag ties for another year. I put the box of mason jars in the blue recycling bin and broke down a few packing boxes whose masking tape was brittle almost completely worn away. I opened the back door of my SUV and after wiping it down, put inside a 1970's Snoopy snow cone machine that I had used with Elizabeth and Bella. There were pieces missing from the Monopoly and Sorry! games that I threw away, the Parcheesi game appeared intact and went into the truck after I brushed the dust off of it. There were a few bungee cords that were brittle from the salt air, a few pieces of loose lumber, and a purple footstool Nono had made for me when I was about ten. The lumber and the brittle cords went into the trashcan, the purple stool into my vehicle, despite the deterioration of two of the four legs.

A large wooden toolbox was next, and I felt my muscles strain as I carried it off the porch. I was like a kid at Christmas that although knowing the contents of that special gift, still couldn't wait to unwrap it. The two rusty latches were unclipped, and the giant lid felt weighted with years. Inside were Nono's tools, tools he and Uncle Sal had used to finish the cellar, tools he made my boot remover with, tools that completed my purple stool. The handles were all wooden and worn with age. There were distinct chips on the metal files, and the level was not quite level. These tools had been used. They had purpose and function, and despite their flaws had produced many practical objects that had taken form in Nono's skilled hands. A baby rocker, a rocking horse, a picnic table, a stool. Pictures were hung and wood trim was replaced. Each tool could tell many stories if granted the power of speech, and most assuredly would tell of strong hands and a firm grip, a sense of determination and a distinct pride in a job well done when finished.

I put the entire box into the SUV, listening as the individual tools moved around. I had to lift one side at a time, the box being too heavily laden with metal pieces of Nono's life. I had no idea what I was going to do with the tools, I had no reason to learn to build wooden benches and dressers...but I found myself totally incapable of parting with his toolbox. Perhaps it was the tactile contact that made the tools come alive in my hand, perhaps it was a pack-rat instinct passed down from my grandmother who had saved baggie ties – but the toolbox had to come home with me, had to remain in my life, had to have meaning for my son, had to exist tangibly, not just in thought and memory.

Years ago, when I was deliberating which direction I would steer my life in, Uncle Sal and Cousin Luca had offered me the opportunity to apprentice under them, learning not only the fix me ups that came with home owning, but enough practical knowledge to make carpentry my career. I had declined their offer at the time, studying political science at UCONN. A degree in Poli-Sci afforded me the opportunity to do absolutely nothing practical, so I returned to school the next year so I could later be unemployed in a more interesting field.

Not that it worked out badly later on. I truly enjoy my work as a Doctor of Psychiatry. I enjoy the patients, the money to afford a decent lifestyle, and there are a few perks of being a doctor, such as being able to park pretty much anywhere I want. But as I lifted the heavy toolbox into the SUV I wondered for a moment if I had not in fact missed out on something special. Had I stayed and learned the trade, would my life have been as happy, happier, or not happy at all? I surely would not have met Susan, and the local girl I probably would have married and passed on her traits to the son or daughter I would have eventually had. This introspection reminded me that things would have been very different. Would I ever have been thinking of alternate futures and different lives or would I have been so content with a life not lived that questions of other realities would not enter my mind? Had my educational training determined my thought pattern as well as my life's goals and values? Had I somehow missed a beautifully simple life that would have kept me somehow closer to this cottage that was preoccupying my current intellectual diversion?

If I had stayed – if I had stayed! Would the cottage have continued differently? Would there even now be voices of children playing and the smell of fresh vegetables in the garden? Would my very presence have kept things from changing so drastically, filling the shoes of Nono as best I could, my youth turning into a patriarchal old age? This I of course could not predict. And as many others before me, I had to realize that the life worth living was the life I had chosen because that was reality.

I moved the few pieces of plastic furniture from the porch, stacking the chairs in the front yard. The porch was now free from obstruction, and I was able to seep the concrete with a push broom that had been left in the corner. I rolled the dry-rotted tire outside and swept the years of dust out of the porch doorway. I went to the side of the cottage and attached a nozzle that I had brought with me to the coiled garden hose. I dragged the hose around the house and onto the porch, then went inside to find some sort of cleaner. The wooden cabinet under the sink still had some lye, Bon Ami, Comet, and Old English furniture polish. I grabbed the Comet and returned to my project, vigorously shaking its contents onto the cement floor. Through dampness and moisture, the powder quality had turned into off-green chunks, but I was able to cover the floor completely. I took the hose and sprayed a mist of water onto the floor and began the arduous scrubbing with the broom. After about ten minutes I noticed some progress in my battle against the grime, and jet sprayed the comet water out the door. The bleach smell mixture made tiny green whirlpools and puddles on the hard ground, the porch still looking concrete-clean but still concrete. I wiped a few beads of sweat off my forehead with my right shirtsleeve.

I went inside and poured myself some red wine that was already a nice cool temperature. Susan should have been picking Antony up about this time, in some place that seemed so very far away. The wine was cool and refreshing and I pulled off a piece of bread and added some Genoa and provolone. There really wasn't anything that quite compared to fresh meat and cheese on fresh Italian bread. My father and I had always carried a loaf when we had gone fishing together, really the most outstanding memory of his stay at the cottage. I don't really know why that's what I remembered most – he really wasn't a good fisherman – but the moments alone we shared on calm seas were always special to me.

We'd always get up just before dawn, sleep still in our eyes and a full day ahead of us. Dad would get the baitfish or night crawlers ready from the day before, and we'd grab the handful of necessary items: a few apples, a gallon of water, a loaf or two of Alonzo's bread, a chunk of cheese and some salami. I'd carry the white Styrofoam cooler and my father would grab the salt-water rods with fifty-pound test. We'd quietly make our way out of the cottage, careful not to let the porch door slam, and walk across the street to the jetty, where we'd find other seafarers already shoving out into the water on small boats with fading red or blue paint.

I remember how beautiful the Atlantic looked as the sun crept over the horizon, the pink and orange rays illuminating the dark blue waters. We never went far enough out as to not see land, but as the sun rose and the tide went out, I felt that I could see eternity. Gulls would follow the more successful fishermen, the locals that began their trade here, selling to small markets all the way up to Waterford. The protection of the cove kept the waters pretty calm and the thought of ever using a motor seemed as remote as not being able to find a school of fish. The waters were teeming with undersea life at this time, and we'd always remark about the position of lobster traps or hail a local with a quick nod and a "morning." These jaunts usually lasted until eleven or at the latest twelve, by that time the sun, having risen to its pinnacle, throwing incredible bursts of heat onto our faces and backs. Gulls cawing, the smell of salt in the air, companionship and always enough fish for dinner. It was simple, and it was a treasure to hold onto. We never minded the blisters on our hands from the oar's rough wood, never minded the constant drifting with the tide and the effort to keep in the channel. It was quality time spent when we'd talk about baseball and schooling, the last catch and the next.

Sometimes we finished with a hand line, the taut string pulling into the skin, making pink indentations that took a few moments to disappear but mostly we used rods and trolled. As I have mentioned already, we weren't the best fishermen, but I wouldn't trade the time spent in the calm open, lost in conversation with my father for anything. Especially after his death a few years ago, these memories became especially precious to me and I retreat to these special moments whenever I need a quick smile. I have lately enjoyed discovering fly-fishing in the cold waters of North Carolina with my son, but those moments on the sea will always be precious.

11.

I was amazed at how long the day was lasting, far and away from the hustle and bustle of my usual daily life. I had walked, cleaned the porch, seen the town and still had hours of daylight to enjoy in this most special of places. I walked out back to where the huge wooden picnic table and benches took up most of the fenced backyard. It was here that family got together, and plates of food always seemed to gather. Three or four generations were always present, laughing, joking, eating homemade pasta and desserts. It was always loud out here, and neighbors would drop in and out, having a piece of fresh fish or some dandelion wine. The only other things in the backyard were a small McIntosh apple tree and Noni's old washing machine.

There was never enough space in the cottage for everyone at any given time, which is why the picnic table in our backyard always seemed to get so much use. The washing machine, hooked up to an outside spigot, was a testimony to the overflowing from the cottage to the yard around it . There was never a dryer, Nono or my father would always hang a simple rope line across the two farthest points in the backyard, usually around the tree and fasten to an eye hook permanently screwed into the cottage's wooden molding. Old wooden clothespins that had no spring mechanism would be gathered in the front of Noni's apron, and one would always be protruding from her mouth, the next pick as she drew a shirt or towel from the small laundry basket she would rest on the picnic table. If we weren't eating, there was usually a load of clothes drying on the line, absorbing the smell of the breeze off the ocean into the clothes' fabric. Dryer sheets that now tout "spring breeze" or "summer's gentle flowers" have absolutely nothing on the smell of freshly picked clothes that had been drying for hours in the warm sunshine. We always found it funny too, when Noni forgot a load on the line overnight where there was a freeze, waking up to stiff ice laden articles that would take another day to defrost and then dry thoroughly.

The apple tree wasn't much of a producer. I'm still amazed that it was able to produce at all so close to the beach. But it did yield a few edible Macs when the wind started to flow cold and I walked over, reaching up and tasting a greenish-red fruit off its lowest branch. Years ago, Bella and I used to drive a couple of hours through the middle of the state just for the feeling of companionship and the liberation of the open road thrusts after teenagers. That's when we'd get the really good Macs, fresh off the trees, picked ourselves using the small wicker-like hard baskets that orchard owners would provide for you. I always wondered how, like the fishermen of the cove, one was able to raise enough of the small product to resell at such a small cost to provide for a family. Even looking out at rows and rows of apple-filled trees, it just seemed farfetched that enough could be collected by one family and sold at market by the pound.

But the apples always tasted delicious, and Bella and I always managed to eat a few more than we should have, our swollen stomachs and inability to move properly, a telltale of where we had been. But those trips were fun, and we'd always return to the cottage with a couple of baskets for whoever happened to be there, usually the youngest of the cousins being the quickest to grab the largest of the apples. Sweet liquid would drip from their small chins, Bella and I wondering how some of the kids could eat apples with teeth missing. The faces were precious. First a squint at the sour Macs' initial bite, then a smile as the lingering fruit became sweet in their mouths. It was a sign that fall was right around the corner, and a delicious one at that.

As I stood there eating the first bites of the sweet-sour apple, the noise from one open window drifted to my ears. It was a ballgame being played out and from what I could make out, it sounded like the Red Sox.

"Martinez at bat, one down, two strikes. Looks like a curve ball from Berry. A swing and a short hop to Dwight Morris for the second out."

They were apparently playing the Yankees.

"Berry's throwing at about 80, first pitch to Morris is low and inside. Ball one." I don't know if it was television or a radio that I was listening to at the moment, but I stopped and paused for a couple of plays, the announcer's clear, concise voice bringing visual impressions to my mind through audible means. My father and I had listened this way on many occasions at the cottage, both of us upstairs sitting in the dark room with only each other and the sounds from an old transistor radio. The batteries were held in by masking tape, and the small handheld device with a spin dial and two-foot collapsible antenna picked up more static than channels.

But we would sit and listen for hours. I'd be lying in bed, in various stages of sleep, and Dad would be sitting next to me in the oversized chair, a glass of wine or RC cola resting on the wooden end table. With our eyes closed and only the radio's sounds, I'd argue as always that we had the best seats in the house. There's nothing quite like visualizing a baseball game through words, just seconds after it happened, your mind trying to conjure into existence what the announcer was seeing and then describing. I guess that's why Wells' War of the Worlds had been so frightening and led not only to his fame, but also to a panicked population in a state of chaos. What was real was about what was pictured, and when the only method of communication was verbal, the mind was free to wander, and it wandered freely.

I knew what each player looked like in my mind long before I had ever seen a televised game. I knew that Nolan Ryan's fastballs were so hard to hit because they moved so fast, and that Pete Rose always slid face fist when stealing a base. Charlie Hustle could bunt and hit and run, and he looked nothing like the rest of the Reds.

Later on, when I'd spend many Saturday afternoons at Fenway or Shea stadium, I'd remember how picture-perfect my mind's eye view had been. I remember telling my father how odd it seemed to watch the players break after every three outs, and then remembered that I was missing the commercial intermissions. The only thing I remember being better at the park was of course the food – a Coca-Cola and a hot dog in a soggy bun that had been in a steamer just a little too long. The hot dog would be in a silver bag, and we'd also get a bag of peanuts in the shell. But taken altogether the taste combination was better than any fine restaurant that I'd ever been in. Maybe it was the cheering crowds, maybe it was spending time with my father, maybe it was the excitement of being in a large city, but everything came together in perfect harmony.

A few times Elizabeth or Bella would join us – Elizabeth preoccupied with people watching (or later on, guy watching), but Bella would enjoy the sport as much as my father and I did. She'd cheer at the long hit balls and yell at the umpire's bad calls, occasionally letting a few choice colorful words escape. After her first divorce, I'd always make sure to take her and Alex to at least a couple of Sox or Mets games each year, Bella turning almost childlike as she entered the coliseum, a ball cap perched with flair on her head, a soda or beer in one hand and her arm locked around mine. Alex would run straight for the closest program barker trading a dollar or five that I had given him for that day's playbook. Later, we'd all dine on those ballpark hot dogs and usually watch the Sox win and the Cubs lose. I wouldn't trade any of these memories for any amount of money. And it all started with a small transistor radio in a dark room on the second floor of a small cottage with my father always resting on a well-worn easy chair. Few things in life are ever this purely simple.

In another nod to the modernization of fast food, I had noticed on my walk earlier this morning that the local pizza place, Little Italy, now offered delivery, something that was unheard of when you had to actually go out to a restaurant to eat their food. Feeling hungry, I went back inside the cottage, looked around for a phonebook and dialed their number on the old rotary dial phone in the small kitchen. The phone was a drab olive color, matching nothing in particular, mounted on the wall to maximize the limited space. Again, it was something practical, not something ornate. The old, coiled cord required me to stand within three feet of the phone, and Little Italy picked up on the third ring.

I ordered myself a large cheese with extra sausage and a bottle of Pepsi-Cola. I was told that it would be delivered in half an hour or so, and the Pepsi was warm, would I mind Coke. I said OK, asked if they took credit cards, and paid for the lunch over the phone. I walked into the main living room, trying to catch part of the ballgame I had heard over the fence while I was outside. A 72" flatscreen with cable had replaced the black and white television that in previous times I had to manually change the dial until I found the game on a UHF station out of New York. The picture was a bit hazy and jumped a bit so I'd give the top of the television a swift rap with my hand and the screen would settle down. I'd then adjust the volume to a pitch that I found acceptable and then sit in the recliner that faced the mammoth sized console.

The chair was larger than the one in the sitting room. This one had been Nono's, and I pulled the wooden handle on the left side to elevate my feet. It seemed like a throw back in time watching the ballplayers hustle around the black and white field with a gray sky as a backdrop. I half expected a Bromo seltzer commercial to appear when the station cut for a break, but a modern drug company's pitchman tried to sell me a sinus relief medication where side effects included dry mouth, fatigue, possible ulcers, and migraines instead. I was assured, however, that the results were the same to those who took a sugar pill, and I probably wouldn't feel any side effects because I wasn't pregnant or a nursing mother.

The game played on, breaking only for advertising, and I drifted out of consciousness a few times. Forty-five minutes later I heard the rumbling of a small car in the driveway that was in desperate need of a new muffler, followed by a crisp knock at the porch door that faced the driveway. I went outside, greeted the pizza driver with the necessary amount of courtesy, and tipped him a couple of dollars. Apparently, the tip was acceptable, or the driver was overanxious, because I received a very hearty thank you sir as the pie was placed into my hands, along with a plastic bag containing my Coca-Cola. I was happy with this, satisfying the delivery driver usually ensured that the next time an order was placed the food was usually delivered while it was still hot.

I went back inside with the hot pizza and cold soda and set a plate for myself on the wooden kitchen table. I poured the Coke into a metal cup, grabbed a few sheets of paper towels from the dispenser and sat down. I opened the pizza box, steam still coming through the air holes on the side and looked at the pie. I immediately realized why a good part of my professional practice dealt with eating disorders and obesity. It looked delicious! The crust was crisp and golden, not the soft gooey crust of the modern pizza chains Americans had become so familiar with. You could tell that this was rolled by hand and baked in a brick oven.

The pizza wasn't perfectly circular, a sure sign that Little Italy still hand-tossed the dough and one bite told me that they still used a three-cheese combination instead of just mozzarella, and despite the change in ownership, the sauce recipe had remained intact. I folded a piece in half lengthwise – the only way any experienced pizza eater could eat a slice, and savored the first, second, third, and each successive bite. The overloaded sweet sausage and liberal amounts of cheese reminded me of when I was a boy and the pieces just looked so huge to me, and one or two slices would fill me.

I ate to the crust and then enjoyed chewing, while also remembering how Noni used to tell us that it was good for the teeth. Like most old wives' tales, that was probably true, the mastication of the tough bread stimulating the gums, and producing a workout for the entire mouth. I decided to consciously stop the scientific explanations of why I was enjoying this meal so much, and instead, focus on another slice, which went down smoothly if not slower than the first. It wasn't quite Noni or Aunt Josie's homemade cooking, but the distinct smell of fresh sauce and oregano, melted mozzarella, provolone and sweet sausage added to the thought of being home once again.

Food was always such a big part of our lives here, whether it was fresh fish, homemade sauce or cold cuts left out all day to snack on and make sandwiches with. I never recall anyone ever getting sick back then from food being left out or reheated, and no one ever complained about having to eat a cold piece of pizza or fried chicken. There had even been a small takeout, the only precursor to the first food chain, here in Branford, where your options for lunch were either a piece of chicken and a scoop of spaghetti or a scoop of spaghetti with a piece of chicken. I think that man's name was D'Angelo and he had built himself a nice house and sent his kids to college on offering this one plate meal to local fishermen and people that just didn't feel like cooking lunch for the kids. His sauce had been more of a mixture of chopped tomatoes and cheap ground beef, but with the piece of chicken and a two-dollar price tag, you just couldn't beat it. He ran this operation out of what could only be described as a shack that was in walking distance to the small pies his wife and oldest daughter were assembling on disposable plates and ringing up a continuous flow of cash. He only had so many pieces of chicken each day and when he was out, he stopped work. Sometimes his shack was open from 10am until two or three in the afternoon but mostly he was able to close up shop around one. The background noise of the game trickled into my ears from the other room. I poured myself some more Coke and took a couple of slices of pie into the living room. At home, this was something that I'd never let Antony do – eating and drinking were confined to the family dinner table, or on Sundays, the breakfast nook where Susan would serve us Belgian waffles and fresh mixed berries or perhaps crepes. But it was different here. It seemed almost unnatural not to walk around the cottage with food in one hand and a drink in the other. There had always been talking and eating around this place, and I settled back comfortably into the recliner as the game played on. This just seemed natural.

“Three up, three down,” the announcer was saying, “and Rodgers retires the side.” I took another bite of pizza. “When we come back, Louis Martinez will face the top of the lineup in the eighth inning.”

Advertisements and a quick station break followed, letting me know from the double look Doppler that the rest of the weekend should be as clear as the past few days. Nothing apparently was happening in the world of much importance, as the teaser for the six o’clock news featured a story about residents wanting to add another streetlight downtown. The intersection apparently had become more dangerous as it became more traveled. I waited for some information about the weather Susan would be having down in Florida, but it was not forthcoming. Besides, the weather channel wasn’t on the list of the three or four basic cable channels the TV could pick up. I remembered that the weatherman for this station had been named Brad Field, which I always found amusing as Connecticut’s only major airport had the name Bradley Field. It was now of course the more impressive sounding Bradley International Airport, or BDL, and I wondered half-heartedly how Mr. Field took the name change.

"And we're back at Yankee Stadium; Yankees ahead five to four." I took another sip of soda and began working on my fourth piece of pizza, feeling wonderfully gluttonous. The pizza was now room temperature and went down without burning my palate. I was thoroughly enjoying this day; pizza and a ballgame being a reward for cleaning up the porch and a life well lived. The Yankees ended up winning the game, and I ended up eating a total of five pieces of pizza, both feats of strength and endurance. I decided to keep the channel set where it was to catch the news, hoping that after the segment on the stoplight, there would be at least something that resembled national news coverage.

After a commercial break, two newscasters, far too young to be taken seriously, appeared onscreen behind a desk that sported a very modern looking station logo and went live to downtown Branford for an update on the traffic light debacle. News-bites followed; a convenience store robbery in New Haven, an appearance by the governor at a birthday party for terminally ill child, and something to do with local fishermen not being able to keep their nets full due to either migration or the past thirty years of overfishing the area.

Brad Field apparently was no longer with this station, as returning from commercial, a very attractive, young blonde offered her take on weather patterns that were emerging throughout New England. As with the other two news anchors, I found myself having a hard time taking her seriously due to her age and Cover Girl good looks, but I was able to decipher the blue lines for cold and the red for hot quite well on my own. Eight years of college had its benefits.

12.

It's hard to imagine how these simple experiences stood out as profound life-altering moments. As a psychiatrist, I've listened to enough people and read enough medical newsletters that dealt with family security and a return to innocence. However, for some reason, I either never thought of myself as impractical as those I treated, or never quite understood the message I was preaching. This comfort, this return, the subject of novels as well as medical journals, was real. I had not so much stepped back in time as stepped back in place. This was the where, regardless of the when. Such simple remembrances from the shore to the pizza – from the toolbox now sitting in the back of my SUV to the gas stove – these simple remembrances somehow almost mystically called forth a comforting past that still seemed to exist, as long as I was in this place.

It was different here. The sounds of children laughing and a lawnmower running could exist anywhere but being held within the confines of this small space, lent special meaning to the familiar sounds and called to mind a plethora of occasions relating directly or indirectly to the object. Here, in this small cottage, my mind was free to wander, free to explore the depths of my own consciousness for once, and not just the consciousness of those around me. The doctor was at last the patient, and this stunning revelation was extraordinary in its inherent simplicity. I had returned – the proverbial prodigal son – but returned to what? Returned to a shell of a house that only provided a backdrop for freely flowing memories? Or was I returning to ruin the castle of Hamlet, my being here setting in motion the end of an age through the vehicle of selling off this property to Tommy Fazio. As an agent of change, what type of change was I bringing to this landscape? History had been kind to those before me. Uncles and aunts and cousins and grandparents – all of whom kept this place sacred to the family – not allowing the world that was passing by outside to alter what was happening inside.

I wondered what type of steward I would be remembered as. Would my son and his cousins remember anything that happened here this weekend? Throughout this life would he point to a specific moment when somehow in some way I played the Judas goat to his inheritance? Would it matter? It seemed to matter to Theresa, her phone call being the first contact we'd had in years figuring prominently in my thoughts. Was this visit a visit I would rue until my death? Would it be added to the events of this family, just as my lifeline was added in scroll to the Bible upstairs? Where would that Bible be, and whose hand would write my life's records if this place no longer existed in time? Would I be responsible for the discontinuation of something that was not only larger than I was, but longer lasting?

I was here to remove the past, to end this stream of existence. Truthfully, I was not wanting this blissful simplicity to end. I wanted this cottage – now more than ever, I wanted to bring my wife and son here and give to them the memories of home that I experienced a generation ago. I did not ask to be thrown into this position of decision making – I was merely a spokesman for the majority of the family. If their wishes include selling off the cottage for a share in a financial windfall – who was I to stop that from happening? I may have been a voice crying in the wilderness, but I was a lone voice. Except for Bella. And now Theresa.

I continued to try and justify my action here in my mind for a few more moments, gave up trying to do so, and ate the last piece of my pizza as the ballgame highlights were replayed on the local newscast's sports segment. I felt rotten inside. I had become my own Ghost of Christmas Past, and I wished that this burden was able to be lifted from my shoulders and placed anywhere else.

The news ended on a predictably happy note, some human-interest story about an immigrant's first trip to the local zoo. My head was swimming with all sorts of thoughts, my mind trying desperately to get into sync with the actions that my body would soon be taking. I needed some fresh air, and automatically began my ascent up the narrow wooden stairs that creaked in all the same places that they had creaked last night. I went into the bedroom I was using on this trip, undressed, and pulled on a pair of swim trunks and put on an old T-shirt with some athletic company's logo on it. I slipped on my beach shoes and headed downstairs. Passing the linen closet, I instinctively pulled out an oversized fluffy white beach towel and headed out the porch door, again, not worrying about locking the cottage, or letting the door slam.

The sun had begun its journey westward, the sky growing steadily darker as I crossed the road and headed for the beach. The tourists had all gone now and only a couple of locals were to be found on the shore. They were mostly older couples out for the relaxing daily stroll that had become part of their everyday routine. There were a few bait men tying up for the night, and their stoic faces betrayed no clue as to their day's success or failure. A few gulls lingered around them, their circular patterns of flight and sound becoming more distant and removed as the sun began to set.

I had always liked a quick dip in the evening waters, the cool salt water and solitude always seemed to cleanse me from whatever troubles I had brought to the cove. I slipped off my t-shirt and beach shoes, swung my arms back and forth to stimulate my senses and get the warm blood flowing and ran into the water, diving in headfirst when I had gotten knee deep. The water was a little cooler than invigorating, shocking my consciousness into a state of intent awareness. I surfaced with a quick gasp, and automatically began swimming away from shore, the motion of my body bringing some warmth as I became acclimated to the surrounding temperature of the Atlantic Ocean in September.

I swam hard and fast, paralleling the coast for a good three minutes, realizing that age and conditioning to another warmer environment had taken their toll on my body. I really was cold. But more than warmth, I needed this. I needed the refreshing waters, regardless of the temperature, to baptize me into a rebirth, to remove my mind and spirit from the unpleasantness of tomorrow's meeting with Tommy Fazio, and to wash away the sins I had believed I would be committing against the memories of my family.

As I had done so very many times before, I stopped swimming and faced the shore, floating just over the ocean floor, my arms in continuous motion against the tide to keep me afloat. Small lights dotted my view from here, the few remaining cottages now relying on electricity instead of the sun to add light to their inhabitants' lives. A few miles off there was a distinct white flare – something I recognized immediately from living in Florida but had never seen here in Branford: ground clutter. The light from what I assumed to be a huge shopping center, and the streetlights they were required to install as part of the deal with developing the land, now cast a light haze in my area of observation obscuring some of the less brightly shining stars that were now beginning to dot the evening sky.

I was cold. Even beyond the physical feeling of the icy sea, I felt cold inside. I swam for a few more minutes, then headed for shore. There was a small breeze blowing and as I reached for my beach towel, I could hear my teeth chattering as I watched the gooseflesh appear on my arms. I dried off as quickly as possible and threw on my t-shirt. My hair was damp, and I could feel the cold sand with my feet as I instinctively buried them for warmth. In an effort to restore some heat to my body, I shook my arms vigorously hopping up and down. I must have been quite a sight to any passerby that would have glanced my way – a broody figure having just emerged from a cold dark lagoon, flailing ungracefully on the shore looking to steal the warmth from any external source.

The hopping and jumping were working. I began to regain feeling in my extremities. I decided to keep consistent with my healthful dip in the ocean and jog a bit down the firmly packed sand. I had done this of course twenty years ago as a college student keeping in shape more for amorous attention than for personal accomplishment, but I had recently restarted this ritual when my size thirty-four pants became so uncomfortable Susan began purchasing size thirty-six. I usually did about two miles a day and leaving my towel near a "Do not dive – shallow water" sign, I put on my beach shoes and began to jog across the sand.

I have always been amazed at how very lost in thought one can become in a nighttime jog, and I found that to be so very much truer on this now desolate strip of beach. There was nothing here – no distractions, no cares – just me and the sound of the rhythmic tide and the slight landing of each footstep on the sand. The stars above had reached their zenith, brightly blazing their long-extinguished light across time and space. I was oblivious to the occasional car that must have passed by. The moon threw a beautiful glare that made my path visible through a cloudless sky. The wind on my face now felt refreshing, not cold despite the drop in temperature, small beads of perspiration formed on my brow. My lungs began to burn slightly as the intake of the evening air filled them to capacity with a distinct chill and I began to notice the vapor mist as my breath cooled in the air at each exhale.

By this time, I had rounded the bend by the farthest jetty that sat across from the Carmichael house, the path ahead becoming darker from the shade of nearby pines that somehow managed to live in such salty soil and extreme conditions. I knew from years ago the proper footing needed to transverse the rock jetty, and intuitively my feet sought out the rocks that would hold my weight without shifting. The jetty was pretty much a mile marker and I automatically slowed down not just for the change in terrain from firmly packed sand to rocks, but I realized that I had a mile to jog back to the cottage.

As I stopped to catch my breath, small clouds escaped from my mouth as I stood there with my hands on my hips walking in a tight circle, I looked out over the cove and let the calmness and serenity of the dark waters come over me. I stood there enjoying a sense of profound peace. I decided to venture out on the jetty, slowly making my way across the rough edges of the coast in a more or less crouching position, owing not so much to my age and lack of familiarity of this place, as to the darkness caused by the pines obstructing the moon's guiding light.

I eased my way out onto the furthest point of the rocky jetty where the water met with external consistency. My hair was still damp and a little cold, so I sat against the wind, knees pulled to chest, arms wrapped around legs. The rhythmic lapping of the slowly moving tide seemed as tranquil as a mother's heartbeat to a child on her bosom. A few dim lights just within my field of vision showed the presence of distant ships, carrying their unknown cargo to unknown locations. Some were undoubtedly making their way northward to a Canadian port, while others appeared to be slowly moving out to sea, traversing enormous distances to finally dock in another English-speaking country.

The lights on the dark water melded with the lights of the dark sky, betraying no separation from water and heaven. The stars, like the ships, were constantly in motion, only their path was slower and more predictable. I rocked back and forth, wanting to enjoy as much of this tranquility as I could before the hardness of the cold jetty took its toll on my back, or the coolness of the evening's air pushed me into motion. A few feet from where I was sitting a couple of small crabs scampered into the water, perhaps in an effort to find food, perhaps becoming food themselves. The sea and all that surrounded it seemed endless and the infinity of what was above seemed matched only by what lived beneath. Countless stars with unknown numbers of planets reflected in this giant pond that housed countless creatures in countless environments. And I was fortunate enough to be sitting here on this pinnacle, a vantage point of observation that would continue into the far future, existing into time when my journey on earth was over, as I was existing here after my forefathers.

The lapping of the small waves continued, and I allowed myself to become lost in their comforting repetition. I had come here many times to think and write as a child, teen, and then young adult. I had come for its beauty and stayed for its effect on my soul. Here I could not only enjoy eternity but experience it. I had written here, stared into the face of God here, fled here when things seemed too tough to bear – and again, predictably, I was here now. I felt somehow drawn to this place like my legs had led me of their own independent will here. I needed to be here where water met sky, and I was.

An overwhelming feeling of conflict overcame me and the realization that my actions after the course of the next two days could eternally change this place began to form in my mind. What would happen to this place began to form in my mind. What would happen to this place when the steady stream of progress bulldozed the cottage and luxury town homes dotted the shores? Would a restoration project eliminate the pine forest behind me and change this jetty into a dock for a marina for tourists and time-shares? Where would the next generation of young people sit and dream about their future, sneak a cigarette, discover the pleasures of a first kiss? In ten years, what would this place look like? Would there be a place to contemplate eternity, or would the hustle and bustle of a tourist community serve up a generation of people immune from the siren-like call of this sea? Was it even my concern? Did my actions actually have a bearing on the very existence of this place? With a shudder due in part to the dropping temperature, and in part to the ominous voice in my head, I realized that yes, my actions would have a direct effect on the very life of this shore.

And so, I sat at the end of the jetty, cold, tired, full of thoughts and despair and darkness, in a place that had always reminded me of love and tranquility, thinking of Poe's "Annabel Lee" in a sepulcher by the sea. I'm not much of a fan of poetry in general, and I consider myself to be a positive person without much interest in the more morbid or depressing aspects of this life. That being firmly established, I will admit to a slight deviation with a substantial interest in the writings of Edgar Allan Poe. I'm not sure from a psychological standpoint, if there is not some deeper interest due to some person or situation that I have not come to deal with adequately, or if it is just human nature to be amazed at the profound, but Poe's simple yet twisted verse has always held a level of fascination for me. Was I not now the protagonist waiting with longing at the side of a shore for some companionship or reconciliation to bring light into my own personal darkness? The character of Annabel returning wasn't physical, it was ethereal – an identification with the past that could somehow rise up from the tomb, shedding light on the gloom of my soul's countenance.

Bella. I needed to talk to Bella. Throughout the day her smile had flashed in mind a hundred times looking at objects that were precious to us together. At the cottage throughout the day, Bella's eyes had sparkled in the pictures of her that dotted the walls of the cottage, her smile brightly adding cheer and love to each room. Such was her effect on me and had always been. I really had resisted calling her despite her proximity to the cottage, not wanting to intrude upon the peaceful lifestyle of the doting Michael that had worked so very hard to create a beautiful life for her and Alex free from day-to-day worries that most people experienced. My call would have certainly introduced an intrusion.

But I felt I needed her. I needed at this moment to be in her reassuring arms, her warmth covering me, shielding me from the ocean's cold. We had sat so many times here, in the summer cooling off and diving beneath a full moon that lit the waters so splendidly, to the dark cold nights like this one, where the very temperature and feeling of isolation had pulled us automatically toward each other. We had talked about everything from schoolwork to vacation plans, new loves to ex-lovers, both of us staring out to sea.

Her eyes were so very remarkable – their crystal blue brightness providing the most wonderful contrast against her jet-black hair and olive colored skin. Bella's eyes danced with kindness, and no one could ever doubt that her interest in them was anything short of truthful. She never had to feign interest in any story. Her attention was always given in totality to whoever was speaking to her. It was as if she were a natural empath responding to whoever was talking to her in the way that was most beneficial to them. And it never felt like an obligation. No matter how long we sat together, arm in arm, hand in hand, I never wanted to move from that place, wherever we happened to be, and perhaps sensing this, Bella would stay peacefully until it was I that began to change venues. Total caring, total submission, total love.

I stood up, noticing a few extra creaks from my body and exhaled a barely audible slight groan. Apparently with age came not only wisdom but also a few side effects that were not quite as pleasant. My jog back from the jetty to my waiting shirt and then to the cottage was quick and faded in a blur. I had a purpose. This wasn't just a refreshing jog or a simple cardiovascular workout; I had a reason to hurry. I quickened my gait, exerting any muscles, oblivious to the dropping temperature, and ran the mile back to the cottage. My mind was already anticipating the call I would make as soon as I got to my cell phone. I completed the run in what was probably my best time since I had run track in college. I hustled across the street and slowed my pace only upon reaching the gravel turnoff that led directly to the cottage's back door. I noticed that the lights were on inside and gave only a momentary thought to the possibility of my not having been the one that had turned them on.

I paced outside for a moment or two, catching my breath and remembering the importance of cooling down after exercising, keeping the body in a state of healthy unrest, gradually slowing it down as opposed to a quick stop. There was the familiar crack of the cottage's screen door and as I looked up, momentarily startled, a wonderful smile crept across my face and engulfed the totality of my very being.

13.

"Coming inside?"

It was Bella! Her small silhouette from the cottage's warm light, the unmistakable searching blue eyes and perfect smile. My heart leapt inside my chest, and a feeling of completion of mind, body and spirit drew me close to her. Laughing, I held her tightly, her warm body providing a dramatic contrast to the coldness I had experienced both externally and internally the last few hours at the shore.

I swung her around, her lightness offering no resistance to the strength in my arms, both of us like children again, her arms draped around my neck, I pulled her close- like a drowning man grabbing desperately for the last life vest in a sea of turmoil and kissed her cheek with tender affection.

"You look great!", I gushed after setting her back down, her face beaming with a hint of red coloration. "Just so beautiful."

And she did look great. Age had been most kind to my cousin; her grown son could easily pass for a potential suitor. Her raven-colored hair was slightly askew from having twirled her with so much gusto, and her laugh at seeing me was infectious. A hundred things and more I wanted to blurt out to Bella – all of them compliments in some way, all of them singing laudatory praises for her beauty of form and preciousness of soul.

"You're wet", she giggled, "and cold, come on inside let's get you warmed up, I'll make coffee or something."

Holding her hand, I allowed myself to be led inside the cottage, closed the door behind me, and looked again at her. She was the type of person you could not help but look at. Her beauty of form was matched only by her beauty of soul, and one immediately realized there was something special about her in her simplicity. She didn't try to be beautiful or kind, caring or attentive - she just was all of these things and more; the classic beauty for whose love wars had been fought over in the mythologies of the past, the present beauty that made young men and old pause in their tracks to stare, and women to either envy or admire.

But my love for Bella was special. It had been a love of a lifetime, starting with our inseparability as small children, leading into our adventures together as young adults, and continuing with an affection that was built over those many years as confidant, treasured best friends – a once in a lifetime meeting of kindred spirits, occupying the same time in existence and recognizing in each other the true meaning of completeness.

“Get yourself some dry clothes from upstairs, and I’ll run the hot water,” she said, walking swiftly toward the shower.

I willingly obeyed, the fact of her just being here with me having filled my heart to overflowing with unquenchable joy. I bounded up the stairs this time, taking them two at a time, increasing my gait to hurry and get back downstairs to where I heard the water begin to flow through old pipes. I grabbed a pair of sweatpants and a t-shirt, some clean underwear and a pair of white socks, and hurried downstairs. My mind wantingto be with Bella that it was almost scared that in any absence I’d find out that she was not really there.

“There’s a clean towel on the rack,” she smiled sweetly, gracefully motioning to the bathroom. “I’ll have some coffee ready for you when you get out.”

I smiled and thanked her. I told her how very happy I was that she was here for about the tenth time and went into the shower. The steam from the hot water making the bathroom appear like a sauna. The water was hot, but felt so good, relieving the dampness of my bones. I stood under the faucet, my body feeling the heat as the water pounded down from my head to my back to my legs. I could hear Bella in the kitchen, filling a pot of water for coffee – she still made it on the stove. I don't ever think the cottage or her house had a drip coffee maker. I began to warm up, literally feeling the coolness of my bones rising through the skin and out of my body. It felt wonderful, and as I turned the old handles off, grabbed the fluffy white towel Bella had laid out for me and dried myself, I felt warm again. I put on my sweats and towel-dried my hair. I exited the bathroom in a cloud of smoke, filling the kitchen with steam that caused the window to fog up slightly. Bella was stirring coffee on the gas stove.

"Swimming at night in the cold waters again," the question with an all-knowing smile.

"You know me too well," I smiled back.

"I never understood your fascination with swimming at night."

"We used to do it together..."

"I was scared! But you loved it!"

I smiled at her.

"You're pink," she said, walking over and brushing my arm with her small hand. "And warm. Still take your coffee light and sweet?"

"Of course. Some things don't change."

Bella looked at me and poured out the dark liquid into waiting cups, added sugar and half and half that she had apparently brought with her, and passed me a steaming cup.

"Just like mama used to make," I said.

"Your mother was a terrible cook, as I remember," Bella jokingly commented as she set the burner on a low flame and pulled up a chair next to mine.

"How'd you know I was here?" I asked, almost burning my tongue with the coffee.

"I called Susan this morning. I hadn't heard from you about the sale of the cottage for a couple of weeks, so I figured you'd be here brooding about it, or out swimming in the ocean."

"Clever girl," I said, unable to take my eyes from hers. They were so blue, so alive, and so very full of love.

"Michael OK? And Alex?"

"Oh, they're fine," Bella smiled leaning gracefully back in the chair, her white sweater and blue jeans responding to her body's motion. "Alex is pitching for a new car – or my car," she continued, a smile on her face.

"I can't believe he's eighteen," I said, more as a testament to Bella's youthful appearance than a recognition of the passage of time. "You both did a great job with him – you have a lot to be proud of." The coffee was now at an acceptable temperature to drink.

I sat silently admiring how kind the years had been, despite the ups and downs, to the features and very countenance of my cousin. Or was it reversed? Had Bella just been kind to the years, turning every situation into an expression of love? She was peering over the coffee cup and instinctively met my gaze with a smile.

For we did love each other, with a love that very few ever experience. A love that transcended time and space, situation and fortune. It was the rare love that inspired poets and dreamers, authors and artists.

As if reading my thoughts, Bella simply smiled and said as a statement of the obvious, "You love me."

I smiled, not at all surprised by the comment and replied, "Of course. I always have. I always will."

She sipped her coffee. "You ever wonder why?"

"For a million reasons, and for one," I said, resting back slightly in my chair, intentionally pausing to respond properly to her directness. "You have always been so dear to me. I don't think I've ever had a time in my life that you were not a part of."

Bella smiled, and I realized with increasing intensity how much she had always meant to me.

"You've always been what I wanted to be. There's a gracefulness about you that just draws people in, Bella. That's why everyone you meet is always smitten by you."

"Smitten," she smiled. "I like that. I thought it was just because I was your favorite." She smiled, a distinct playful banter in her speech.

Catching on immediately to her playful jest, I took a sip of coffee before I continued. "You are special, you know. You have a gift that draws people to you and keeps them there."

Bella reached out and held my hand as I struggled for words. Her hand fit perfectly in mine, her soft skin and natural warmth sending an electric current throughout my entire body. Looking into her eyes, I knew exactly why I loved her so much.

"What is it?" she asked.

"The real reason. The reason aside from the time together, our closeness and everything – the reason that no matter what, you have my heart."

"Maybe I shouldn't know. It would be a lot to keep living up to."

"That's exactly it," I said. "No matter what you do, no matter where you are, you don't have to live up to anything. I love you for being you. Out of all the people that have come into my life – Susan, Antony, my dad and mom, even Elizabeth – you are the only one that never disappointed me, that has never let me down."

There was a distinct pause as Bella digested my revelation. After a moment of reflection, her whimsical smile returned. "Maybe you set too high standards for everyone else. Maybe you don't expect as much from me as you do from them."

I smiled at her and kissed her hand. "Actually, the fact is I expect more of you than anyone else. I have only ever wanted you to be you, and I have just loved you for who you were. You have always been yourself...and it is a beautiful self that I see every time I look at you."

A look of peacefulness and comforting love swept across Bella's face. "Thank you," she said. "I almost think that you love me even more than Michael does."

"I do, "I said without hesitating. I don't put any conditions on my love for you. It's absolute. Michael is wonderful and it thrills me to know how well he treats you, but a husband-and-wife relationship always has its ups and downs, and by nature is conditional."

Bella smiled and laughed. Not loudly, but a laugh, nonetheless. I looked puzzled at her laughter, so she began, "You are the psychiatrist! I love it when you look so deep into everything and come up with the simplest of answers. We really do care for each other," her smile was positively radiant, and I returned it with enthusiasm.

"Why are you here, Vincent?"

"You know why, Bella. I've got to sell this place. I've been elected by age and gender to sell off this place to the highest bidder and divide the spoils equitably between the surviving parties."

"Now you sound like Theresa," Bella said. "Are you sure you aren't a lawyer, too? I've heard psychiatrists are a pretty smart bunch of people."

"Thanks. I've always wanted to remind people of being a lawyer." I faked a look of dejection.

"You know I'm kidding – but you still haven't answered my question, doctor lawyer. Why are you here? I know that your broker is coming here out of professional courtesy. There is no reason for either one of you to be here. You're not selling a used car. Mr. Fazio – I think that's his name..."

I nodded my assent.

"Mr. Fazio isn't going to kick the tires and take it for a test drive. He's buying the cottage to tear it down and put up some condos so the new upper class can have a nice high rise to stay in when they bring their boats up from Florida."

She was correct, of course. Like my cleaning the porch this afternoon, my entire trip to Branford was in reality, quite pointless.

Bella again reading my thoughts, "You need to be here for the same reason I needed to be here."

"What reason is that?" the doctor asked the patient.

"This cottage and everything that's happened here is part of who we are. We will never leave this place in its entirety, and there is a part of you that would do anything to turn back the clock thirty years or so and relive each and every moment you spent here, regardless of whether it was a good time or not. It was still something, and you are not ready to give up something for nothing. You have a connection to this place just like you have a connection with me. You love me. You love this place. I have always been a part of this place, so you love it even more. Nono, your father, Uncle Sal, Uncle Gino - all the role models for masculine behavior have passed through this place and left their mark here. You want to do the same for your son, my son, and the rest of the cousins. You are feeling slighted that your time up to bat has the coach telling you to walk, or at least to bunt. You're not ready to retire your uniform and despite the wishes of the rest of the family, you're not ready to quit this place."

I sat there in purposeful silence, staring at my cousin as this flow of words escaped her lips in a very matter of fact way. It was a statement, a reasoned discourse...and what she said was right. I wasn't ready to quit this place. This had been my home. I had always imagined myself taking on the role of Nono or Uncle Sal, my father or Victor as I grew older. I wanted my children to spend weekends here with their cousins, enjoying the laughter and unrestrained joy that was to be had here. I desired that my family's family would recall how I had labored in the cellar, how I had thrown festive reunions, how I had taken the kids clamming in the morning and shrimping in the evening.

Bella sat across from me and smiled, taking another sip of coffee. She stood and silently went over to the stove, retrieved the warm pan, and filled my cup then, hers. She mixed both of our coffees, put the pan in the sink, and turned off the burner. Moving to the sink, she began to wash the pan and the few dishes I had used that afternoon. I stared with wonder at her, my eyes not leaving her for a moment.

She still had her back toward me as she spoke, "Was I close?"

"Closer than you know." I took a sip of the hot coffee and continued to stare at her.

"You want things to be how they were or at least how you remember them to be."

"There's a difference?"

"Everything gets romanticized over the years. I think as we get older the past becomes more appealing, especially when there's a place like this that you can escape to in your mind."

"But they were good times, Bella."

"Of course they were," she turned to me, "remember I'm the one who opted not to sell this place when the idea first came up."

"I know. I just feel the weight of the world on my shoulders."

"Good thing you have big shoulders." She smiled and came over to me, kissed me on the forehead and began to massage my neck. I instinctively leaned back and let this quiet pleasure relax me thoroughly, as it was no doubt intended to do so. I closed my eyes and tried the visualization exercises that I was in the habit of describing to my patients. *You are in a favorite place. Someone you love is with you. You are totally in that place, totally relaxed and totally living what you are now experiencing.*

The ironic part of this was that the place I always went to in my mind, that favorite place with my favorite someone was right here. The cottage and Bella had always been my anchoring points, the place I went to when I was stressed or could not fall asleep. I was thinking of this place with this someone while I was here and with her. The difference was that after tomorrow afternoon at 4 p.m., I'd only be able to come back here in my mind. I could never return again here physically and despite my cousin's soothing touch, a pang of sadness crept into my heart.

"I'm staying here tonight with you," Bella said, pulling me out of my self-imposed introspection. "I already set up Noni's room, and if it's ok with you I'll make a quick sauce, and we can have some noodles. I've already told Michael and he and Alex are going to have a guy's night out. I hope that's okay with you."

Bella turned around waiting for me to answer. "I think it would be OK, I guess," I said in a teasing manner, got up and hugged her.

Returning my hug, she asked me to get out a couple of pots and began quickly dicing the onion and garlic she must have brought with her. She put a few drops of olive oil in a warm skillet and added some sausage along with the spices. The cottage filled with the delicious aroma of fresh sauce as she emptied two cans of whole tomatoes and a can of paste into Noni's large metal pot. She moved quickly and with purpose as she stirred the frying sausage with one hand and added seasoning to the tomatoes with her other. A piece of salt pork was added to the tomatoes as they began to cook down. I offered to help every so often, only to be lovingly rebuffed. She enjoyed this part of life – taking care of someone she cared about.

I thought again of how fortunate Michael was, able to come home every night to Bella's obvious charm and manners, enjoying along with

Alex, the total attention and affection of a beautiful woman. Although we had never quite seen eye to eye, and a small degree of distrust was evident between us, I could never fault him for his choice in women and could only admire his being able to secure Bella's complete affection. He was good to her, a very loving stepfather, offered her some degree of financial comfort (she never had to work) and really was interested in her well-being.

Which all made me wonder why exactly I really didn't care for him. Had I been anyone else, say a patient of mine, presenting myself with such a situation, I would immediately declare that the emotion was jealousy, a base emotion that I felt far above in my personal development. Yet as I watched Bella move throughout the cottage, what other emotion could I really ascribe to my unwanted displeasure in her husband? Yet here I was, in my forties, well-educated and reasonable, wanting to leap up and down like a child when given a commitment by Bella to spend the night. And here I sat pondering what hold she had on me that would cause me to experience this perceived emotion of profound reflection, she had said it earlier and with conviction. I loved her. I loved her so much that I wanted her for myself, being able to enjoy moments of laughter and joy that I had only experienced in her presence. Michael was a very fortunate man, and maybe it was about time that I started to realize his good intentions – he had proven them consistently enough throughout the past ten years of their marriage – and accept him for what he is - a good man who married well. I looked at Bella. Very well. He married very well.

I set the table for the two of us, using the rose trimmed dishes that Noni had purchased with S&H green stamps years ago, another relic from the past, giveaways from grocery stores and gas stations in the 60's and 70's. I tore off a couple sheets of paper towels as Bella boiled the water for the noodles and poured two glasses of red wine and two glasses of water. I used a serrated knife to cut the bakery bread, arranging five pieces on a wooden basket on top of a paper towel, and laid out the forks and spoons.

Bella had brought a head of lettuce and I chopped it, putting equal portions in two worn bowls, also having the rose pattern. I found a bottle of red vinegar and put it on the table along with the olive oil, then drained the noodles in the sink, the hot steam rising quickly to my face. Bella ladled sauce on the noodles and placed a generous helping on my plate and a small amount on hers. We held hands as we repeated the standard prayer asking God to bless the gifts that we were about to receive and began our meal.

The sauce was wonderful as always and without too much trouble I eagerly finished my plateful as well as a couple pieces of bread. Pausing for conversation and a few sips of wine, the experience was wonderful. It had been years since Bella and I had enjoyed a meal between the two of us without interruption from children or spouses. I added some oil and vinegar to my lettuce and finished the salad over a second glass of wine. When I was done, Bella took up another serving of pasta for me, adding a second ladle of sauce to its top. She ate slowly and lightly, her small frame content with only a portion of the food it needed, especially considering how wonderful it tasted. Susan had never really gotten the knack for preparing a good sauce, her cooking skills in general leaning more toward take-out and restaurants than home-cooked meals. Bella, on the other hand, was at home in a kitchen, making it quite her own in just a few minutes. Knowing that I was overeating brought a smile of pleasure to her face...my having a third helping, albeit smaller than the first two – a testament to how good the meal was.

"Delicious," I said, leaning back and wiping my face, checking to see how much sauce had ended up on the front of my shirt.

"You could hardly tell," she said, reaching over and dabbing sauce from my cheek that I had missed.

"I haven't had sauce in ages," I said, wondering how the button on my pants was staying fastened. "This was really great. I wish Susan could whip up a meal like this."

"Susan's sweet, honey. She just has a lot on her plate. A lawyer's life doesn't really lend itself to domestic concerns – I get to stay home and practice, you know."

"You're very kind. She doesn't have to work. She could stay home and cook me pasta."

Bella laughed. "Susan would be climbing the walls within a week. She's a brilliant lawyer. You could stay home and cook. I seem to remember you making some pretty good meals for me when we lived together after Jordan and I separated. I used to love your cooking."

"I loved cooking for you," I said matter-of-factly. "That was a great time for me. I know it wasn't the best all around, with the custody fight and everything, but I can't help but smile when I think of those years."

Bella smiled appreciatively as she dried her hands on an old towel. "I loved those times too. Every day felt meaningful. I used to love getting up and seeing you off to work. You'll never know how much it meant to me and Alex that you stepped in and took care of us. Alex needed a father figure, and I really needed some shoulders to lean on. The time went by so very quickly though, especially after you started seeing Susan again."

There was a pause in which I recognized a sense of having perhaps somehow missed something that from a practical point, could never have been more than it was, even though then, as well as now, seemed to be everything.

"I'm just glad we had those times," I continued softly, and somewhat lamely, groping for the right words to say to my cousin.

Bella gave one of her signature smiles that said in a glance that everything was not only alright but how it was supposed to be. She reached over and took my hand in hers. "Let's go sit outside," she said, "unless you're still too cold from your swim earlier."

"I think the pound of spaghetti I inhaled warmed me up quite nicely," I replied. "Let me run upstairs for a second and get a cigar."

"I thought you quit smoking."

"I have, but once in a while I just want to taste the sweetness of a cigar."

"Must be a guy thing," she said. "I never understood how you all would smoke those things."

"Uncle Sal's was the worst," I offered. "Remember those foot long stogies he was always chewing on? I couldn't stand the smell. At least Dad's and Nono's smelled like cherries."

"Is that what they were supposed to smell like?" she teased. "I used to gag every time one of them lit up. Still, I remember it and them sitting outside drinking amaretto or some other liquor while the rest of us girls stayed inside and cleaned up."

"All except you, of course. You were always out with me."

"Of course. It's a wonder I have any domestic skills at all. I enjoyed it outside with you so much more. It was much more fun than 'Isabella, dry the plates, or Isabella, get coffee for Victor'."

I smiled and told Bella I'd be right back. I went upstairs, found the pack of Swisher Sweets in the side compartment of my travel bag, located my lighter with my initials on it, a gift from Susan about ten years ago, and with a very full stomach descended the stairs. Bella was already sitting outside on the front stoop, having put on a fleece sweatshirt and a thick pair of socks. I opened the porch door and sat next to her, the cold air immediately hitting my face. It was late, but far too early to sleep, especially with Bella here –

every second we spent together was precious to me, I didn't want to miss any of them.

"Hey," she said simply as I sat down next to her. I immediately put my arm around her shoulder for mutual warmth. "Hey back," I said, unwrapping the package of cigars and lighting one, the smooth cherry taste leaving a pleasant aroma in the still night air.

Bella was quiet for a moment and then said, "Uncle Gino always used to smoke those."

"I remember. He was something."

"He would have been," her breathing leaving vapor.

I continued to smoke the cigar. "He did the right thing; it was just the wrong war."

We were quiet for a few minutes letting our thoughts catch up with the present. Uncle Victor had his medals mounted and framed, along with a picture of Uncle Gino in his white marine hat with the gold insignia. It's really a lovely tribute to him and Noni had kept the matted piece prominently featured to the left of the door, a constant reminder of her son's life and death. The picture was still there, and I made a mental note to remember to take that with me, along with the crucifix that hung over the door. Some memories should remain. His was one of them.

14.

I came back to my present surroundings after the mental diversion to find my cigar almost burned out and Bella looking at me quizzically. I smiled at her with slight resignation and took a pull from the cigar, relighting it. Bella was searching my face with her beautiful blue eyes trying to understand where my mind had been.

"Uncle Gino," I said. "You're right, Noni would have rather had him outlive her." We were silent for some time, enjoying each other's body warmth, commenting absently on how beautiful the stars looked and how bright they were from this vantage point. I told Bella of my trip into town this morning, the changes I'd noticed in Branford and asked her how long it had been since she had come to the shore.

"We haven't been this year," Bella said, her arm wrapped tightly into mine, "but we've managed to stay for at least a week or two every year. Alex really gets a kick out of girl watching at the beach now that he is in high school, and he's managed to make a few extra dollars now and then delivering pizza and doing some yard work. Jimmy Carmichael usually hires him to rake leaves or something- Alex would probably do it for free. Jimmy's got a daughter Alex's age that's really a pretty little thing. She's got herself a steady boyfriend, but you'd think she was the only girl alive to hear Alex talk about her. I honestly don't know if I could stand hearing more than two weeks of it," she concluded with a smile.

"Ah, the rites of spring played out along the shore," I remarked with mock sagacity: "I seem to remember many a suitor appearing on the doorstep of this cottage whenever you used to visit."

"I'm aghast!" she joked back, "besides, it's different – this is my son...that makes me old!"

"Yeah, all the neighborhood kids keep talking about what a babe Alex's mother is."

Bella punched me lovingly as she let out a small laugh, she knew it was true.

I lit another cigar as I put an old towel on the concrete stoop on which we were sitting. The coolness of the step had begun to creep up my spine.

"Really making up for lost time with the ceegars, huh senor?"

"It's peer pressure. I just wanted the girls to think I was cool."

"You're cool alright," she said, watching the smoke from the cigar drift heavenward. "I miss this time together," Bella reflected. "I used to wait all summer for your folks to get here. It was so boring with only the girl cousins. They always wanted to do something at the beach then they had to go into town at night to troll for guys along Main Street. I couldn't wait for you to come here so we could do something fun, anything. All of our adventures real and imagined..."

She started to drift.

"I was so happy every time we pulled up and saw you come to the car. Elizabeth always seemed to get a little moody on the trip, well, maybe that's just how brothers and sister sharing the backseat of an old station wagon behaved – restlessly."

Bella answered with poignant honesty, "I think she was a little jealous of the time we spent together. She was never quite old enough to be included in anything other than whatever the young girls were doing. Elizabeth's smart though. I sometimes feel like I monopolized all her time with you."

"Scarred for life," I kidded.

"No, I'm serious. Your sister really does love you, Vincent. She's always just been in your side vision."

"I haven't talked to her in over a year," I lamented. "I send her kids birthday presents and gifts for Christmas, but I feel like I'm a million miles away from her."

"She took your dad's death pretty hard. She was really close to him, and I think the fact that you and he weren't really on speaking terms angered and frustrated her."

I took another pull off my cigar and exhaled audibly. She was right and she knew it. I know it too, and I knew that she knew that, too.

"No, I can't really blame Elizabeth, I just would really like to have a relationship with her and the kids – what are their names again..."

"Stop that!" Another slight punch followed by soft laughter. "She'll come around. She just never saw...well, you know."

"Yeah. She never saw the crap I had to live through."

We both sat in total silence, Bella's sweet laughter fading unceremoniously away into memories that I had spent a lifetime repressing.

"He was a sick man, you know" she offered up after a minute or two went by. He couldn't help all his actions."

"I know, and sometimes I feel more pity than hatred towards him. But some things are hard to let go of. When he was taking his medication, he was fine, but you know what he was like when he was off it, especially after my mother left him." I was rambling on a bit, so I stopped and took a pull off the cigar that was slowly burning itself down towards my fingertips. Bella had her head on my shoulder, but wasn't forthcoming, so I continued my monologue.

"He was funny, but hateful; he'd give you the shirt off his back one moment and be screaming like a banshee the next. He was magnanimous to those that knew him casually but to those of us that lived with him he was demeaning and unforgiving. I could never do enough right and I guess that's one of the reasons Elizabeth and I don't see eye to eye. He was gentle with her. I was his sounding board and felt the wrath of his anger where she just got the gifts and affections of his generous side. It was almost as if there were two of him living at home, and I always served to get the Mr. Hyde side of his character." My fingers began to get warm, so I flipped the cigar butt into the bushes.

"You went through a lot. A lot more than anyone should have," Bella said. "I felt so bad for you when we'd come visit. I could see the anger building up inside of him and I could tell that you were going to get the brunt of his anger after we left. There were times when my mom would stay an extra day or two at your house just so that his anger would cool off and he wouldn't be so bad with you and your mother. She was a saint to put up with him for so long – she couldn't have been all that happy. I think it was more for you and Elizabeth than it was for her. I think that your mother wanted you guys to have as close to a normal childhood as you could have considering your father's disposition."

"Yeah, I always thought it was a mistake for them to stay together for us kids, and she's told me that in retrospect she should have left him sooner. Her generation just took so much and expected so little from men."

"Maybe that's why you're the way you are," Bella offered quietly.

"Are you saying I'm nuts too?" I jokingly asked in response.

"Silly. You know what I mean – you have a tremendous amount of patience, and have always been good with people, even before you went off to become a doctor. People like you, and I think you are one of the most even-tempered people I've ever met."

I let her kind words sink in for a few moments. "Thanks Bella. I have my moments, but I really think that people that grow up like I do can either go one way or the other. I could have been exactly like my father or do my best to be totally opposite. I choose every day not to be like him. Not just for my sake, but for Susan and Antony and everyone else that I come in contact with. I can't be like him."

"You're not," she said simply. "You are wonderful and caring and giving and loving. Don't even think you are like your father. The only thing

I can see that you inherited from him is how smart you are. He was pretty sharp."

"I'll give him that," I said. "Unfortunately, most of the battles weren't battles of wits. I would probably have lost those too, but it probably wouldn't have been so painful."

Bella simply smiled at me knowing sometimes that it's better to leave some things unsaid, and not to bring into consciousness some things that were perhaps better left alone. "Want to walk?", she said to me after a pause in which I began to contemplate some of my father's ways and means.

"Yeah," I said with an air of resignation mixed with finality, "let's let sleeping dads lie."

Bella cringed out loud and taking my hand in hers as we had done hundreds of times before, sprang to her feet and headed down the driveway. The grass had almost frozen, so the dew point evened out and the cool temperatures settled in for the night, causing our steps to produce a barely audible cracking noise, somewhat akin to stepping on pine needles in a quiet forest. Because of the season, the time of night, and the chill, we were the only two out along the road, heading north along a once well-traveled gravel path.

If she felt the cold that I felt in her hands, she never let on, and since I had always been convinced that her warm heart fueled her with energy that was a part of life itself, I assumed that she was comfortable and happy. For my part, I was ecstatic. I was spending time with someone who loved me so completely, for who I was; a woman that had shared the highs and lows, the laughter and the tears with me my entire life. Bella was my anchor in reality and as we silently approached the old softball field, now overgrown with weeds and neglect, I realized that my being here was significant for her life too.

The impending sale of the cottage was a major event in her life, and any happiness or despair would not only be felt consciously through her but would be felt in actuality by my beloved cousin. That was the reason for Theresa's call earlier, and to some extent, Bella's visit. I knew that Theresa would not have called without some impetus that had brought to consciousness a very real situation of a strong emotion, but Bella would have come just because I was here, just to visit me by the shore. And that was the point. After the cottage was gone, we couldn't have this.

Yes, we could meet at her house like Susan and I did every couple of Christmases or we could invite her and Michael down to Florida and visit some theme park with a few thousand other families... but this would be lost forever. Not the closeness or the holding of hands, not the memories of simpler times and simple pleasures, but the apex at which memories and the physical world met, the central point of shared realities that brought us all together, year after year, life after life.

We shimmied over an old seawall and stood looking out across the dark sea, two figures at once alone on our empty planet, and at the same time, as connected in time and space with all who had ever lived. Bella had her hands and arms around my waist, and I was hugging her with my left arm while my right hand was in my pocket. "It's beautiful," she said, looking up to where God's feet rested on his heavenly throne. "So peaceful, you forget it sometimes when you're away from here and going about the daily routine of cooking meals and shopping for clothes and picking up kids for hockey practice. But it's always here every time I've come, just waiting for me. It's like I never left. Every time, every year, it's just as I left it," she smiled.

It felt wonderful to hear Bella's voice, to stand here with her, listening to casual remarks about her life, interrupted with the sounds of small waves lapping the sand only a few feet away. Her touch was warm and wonderful, in perfect harmony with the fresh salt air. If ever one could truly have a moment of pure contentment, a tangible, non-abstract feeling of being engulfed by comfort and love, this was such a moment. I was glad the moment was with her, and I was glad that I could recognize it for what it was. It literally meant the world to me, to stand here in the cool night air with the person who had so affected my life, so become the focal point of my happiness. This moment, this here, this now – that was all that mattered to me in the world... and it was enough.

But would I have this now if I had not had the experiences throughout my life with Bella, personified in this place, and in the cottage? Would I be where I was now, in a recognizable moment of perfect bliss without the years of togetherness spent on the shore? I knew the answer had to be no, for each life experience adds or subtracts its own character in each person's life – and I started wondering if I was in some way robbing my son and future generations of such boundless potential peace. In my striking the final blow against the cottage, allowing it to pass out of the family – then be destroyed – was I not also striking a mortal blow against my own son, against a future that was limitless as the sky and sea that stretched out before us?

"Brrrrr....", Bella said as she shuddered briefly as the wind began to pick up a bit. "It's going to get cold tonight. I'm glad I brought an extra quilt – I didn't know if the gas heater was running or not." I responded that I'd already checked it out and assured my cousin that we had at least another week of propane left. Bella simply smiled and we began to walk down the beach under the light of a full moon.

"I love being with you," I said with a simple honesty that reflected the depth of my feelings for Bella. "Every time we are together – especially here – time slips by so very fast, and yet it seems so eternal. I don't even know how to explain it."

"You.... lost for words?" she joked, squeezing my hand.

"Hard to believe, I know," I replied as we continued walking away from the cottage at a purposely slow pace. "I get lost here with you."

"I know. I've seen it in your eyes for the past fifty years."

There was a twinkle in her eye that I caught in the moon's glow. I laughed-not loudly, but just loud enough to be heard. "It's true," she continued, "It's that once in a lifetime feeling of pure love that simply just is. I know it because I feel the same way about this place. That's the reason we are walking out here hand in hand at eleven thirty at night on a deserted beach instead of being at home with our families watching a Star Trek rerun or the news." I laughed a bit louder.

"I've missed you," I said.

"No, you've got me. You've always had me. I think that's the reason you and Michael have never seen eye to eye. He knows that no matter how much I love him- and I love him with all of my heart- there will always be a special love that you and I share that is somehow different, yet more than I could give to him. We are here now because of the special place our hearts share at moments like this."

"I thought you were here to talk me out of fulfilling my duty by selling the cottage," I said half mockingly.

Bella became serious: "No. I'm here to make sure that you can live with whatever decision it is that you make in the next few days. I'll still love you. Elizabeth will still love you. So will Susan and Antony. I'm just here to make sure you still love yourself."

"It's not easy," I said.

"I know that, sweetie. It's a lot of responsibility for you because you actually care. Me too. The ones that want to sell are the ones that can't remember or choose not to. I don't know why it's more important to us, but I know that it is."

"So many things have happened here that have made me who I am," I offered. "I have so very many memories – learning how to drive, my first kiss...playing with the Carmichael kids. The

Sunday meals, Noni…. this place was my childhood."

"And it was safe for you."

"That's probably why Theresa called. This place was safe for her too, and she found the cottage the one comforting place she could always return to. She had a vested interest in the cottage physically being here, even if she doesn't visit or include it in her conscious life. Somewhere, back wherever it is that her mind goes back to- this place is safe for her, and she doesn't want this place to cease being. Theresa needs this place to always be here-just like we do, but for different reasons.

"We all have our own reasons, Vincent."

"What's yours?"

We stopped walking and Bella faced me. "It's closer to your reasons than Theresa's; more of a fondness than a place of escape. I always feel the most alive here. You were a big part of that, the two of us doing everything together each summer and on holidays. I laugh every time I think of the little things. Like all of us younger cousins under the table at someone's wedding or graduation with our own jug of cheap wine, pretending we were so grown up. Sitting under a buffet table so no one would see us! I think of how much sheer fun everyone had here, adults and kids alike. Your mother loved this place…she was a nut! I'd laugh every time she'd try to tell a story. I can't remember one she actually finished. She got so sidetracked and flustered. She was the world's worst joke teller, but she was a riot watching her entertain herself! And it was all so very good-natured. We'd all laugh so hard at her, but she always knew it was never mean-spirited..she'd laugh right along with us at herself, having just as much fun as the rest of us."

"She really was a good egg..." I said.

"And she's where you get your sympathy from. No matter how rotten your father was to you, or how demeaning he was to her, she was always able to laugh here and take the good parts of life home with her."

I sighed, "I always thought that was so sad."

"Parts of it were. But she really loved you and Elizabeth. She's always been my favorite Aunt. Not because of any gift or special treatment, but because of her personality and her plain kindness to other people. I don't think she had a mean bone in her body, and I was so glad that she was able to remarry after she left your father. It took courage to do that, a courage that she never let show until the divorce. I still haven't met her new husband, but whenever I talk to her, she seems so happy and relaxed.

"There's part of me that wishes she would have left my father a lot sooner. I'm not quite sure of the merits of staying together for the sake of the children."

Bella: "I think that's generational, and I also think it's very human. It took me years to get enough courage to tell Jordan I had had enough. It's hard to be a woman and realize that everything you've been trained to want is not what it's supposed to be. Especially when there are children involved. I wanted to have a father figure for Alex. I needed that every bit as much as he did. I was fortunate enough to have you. Then when things started to become serious with Michael, I knew that I could truly be happy, and my son could be happy too."

"I guess leaving is easier for men," I said. Every couple I've ever counseled that ended up splitting always seems to be more difficult for the woman. Not just emotionally, but in a practical sense. A single guy that only has to play Dad every other weekend can still work, keep the same job, and find other activities. It's the woman who must cope with doing more while having less."

"Absolutely. A woman has to find a sitter who usually makes more an hour than the woman in her traditionally low-paying job. She then has to watch and wait for that monthly check that hardly covers the true cost of child support, as well as worrying about getting a bad reputation if a man falls into her life. A woman with a child is also considered easy prey because of her desperate situation."

"Not too good in the fairness department."

"Nope, but that is the reality of the situation.... By the way, I'm freezing out here, you wanna start heading back to the cottage yet?"

"I'll follow wherever you go.," I said, not wanting to miss one moment of the time we were spending together.

After a quiet turn heading back to the cottage, Bella asked, "Do you see her often?"

"Who, my mom? No, not really, ever since she got remarried, we kind of drifted away...phone calls every week, then twice a month...Now with her agreeing to sign off on the cottage sale I guess I feel even more distant. Elizabeth is close to her though; the kids are loving growing up so close to their grandmother." The wind was cold on my face.

"I've yet to meet her husband...Don, isn't it?"

"That's him all right, and despite myself, I ended up really liking him."

"Are YOU trying hard enough?" she asked in the non-judgmental style that made my cousin so easy to talk to.

"Probably not," I admitted, "But it's hard. I don't mind them being together, especially if it makes her happy. She had more than enough garbage to dump when my father left, but this guy was just so gruff to anyone except my mother. We're all happy for her, but we just needed some time to adjust to her new life."

Bella was quiet for a moment as we quickened our pace back to the cottage, our heads bowed low against the cool wind. A slight mist stung our eyes, but we couldn't tell if it was a cool rain or an updraft from the sea sending tiny droplets of saltwater horizontally against our forward motion.

We passed back over the ball field. I remember being young and spending a lot of time there with my father. Yet another memory turned sour because of his personality and his demands. I was never enough for me just to play ball and have fun, I had to play ball to win. And winning meant practicing and since I was a catcher, it was important to learn to take a few hits and learn how to catch barehanded. I remember the initial pain followed shortly by numbness as the pink color of my hand would inevitably turn red as they began to swell. I'd hear him yelling at me to stay in front of the ball…" block it with your body…if it gets past you, it's over! Block it! Stop crying like a baby. Get in front of the ball. Be a man!"

I unconsciously grabbed Bella's hand tightly, silently praying that she would not notice the icy tear running down the side of my face. These were memories that I shared only with her, and she would instinctively understand the pressure I was applying to her small hand in mine. "It's OK," she said.

"Yeah," I said, continuing to crossover to the old gravel path. "Some things are just harder to cope with than others."

"Some things I don't think you have ever dealt with Vincent."

"Probably not. I'm not much of an advocate of reliving past experiences that were painful."

Bella smiled sweetly, "It might help you feel better about your father's death."

"You know it's still bothering me?", I ventured.

"Of course. But you're the one that's the big shot psychiatrist at three hundred dollars an hour.... I just make dinner and do the laundry," Bella teased.

"I could analyze your inferiority complex for a very reasonable rate..." I laughed back.

Bella hit my arm, "Thanks a lot," she smiled, her gentle punch in the arm reassuring me that everything was indeed OK, or eventually would be.

We got to the driveway that led up to the cottage, the lights were still on. "I'm so cold!" Bella said, blowing on her cupped hands as she brought them to her mouth.

"But you're cute blue..." I said to her simply.

"Yeah... another thing I can't help... let's get inside and warm up! I could sure use a hot toddy and a warm blanket."

We went inside the cottage, and I locked the front door behind us, more for Bella's sake than anything else. The door could have probably stayed unlocked all winter and everything would still be here when the first summer visitors arrived at the shore. Now kids would pull up into the driveway without their parents, each looking expectantly outside for their favorite cousin or best friend from down the street.

I took a moment and realized the implications of my actions during the next few days. No more Sunday dinners of spaghetti and sausage, no more Friday fish dinners. No more Christmas presents piled high under Noni's silver Christmas tree, no more sounds of children running up and down the creaky stairs and their parents telling them to take the commotion outside. The trips would stop. The social intercourse would disappear. The memories of this place would fade over time as they had already started to do.

No one would remember the birthdays of second cousins, no one would remember having bought the silver tree because of a squirrel in the year before's real pine. No one would remember the fresh lobsters from Mystic or the train trips into New York from Hartford. It would all simply fade slowly...and then it would be gone.

15.

I turned on the gas heater and listened for the predictable ticking noises as the old copper pipes warmed up. The radiator was a huge relic of a time before all emphasis was placed on the idea that an item of quality had to be small. Everything was built big and seemed to last forever. From the five-foot metal radiator to the twenty-seven-foot Oldsmobile Noni used to drive with the chrome bumpers and heavy doors, everything seemed to be made of metal and built to withstand accidental bumps or falls. There was no ten-dollar coffee maker bought at a local mega store, the coffee was made in a pan on the huge stove. TV sets were huge wooden consoles, and buildings went up instead of spreading out, and you only dieted for weddings and graduations. Being bigger was equated with being better; size meant strength.

This was of course before the arrival of the computer and the processing chips. It was a time before environmentalists protested about gasoline consumption. TV sets began shrinking to screens only, telephones became mobile (and then smaller) and cars that would have fit in the Oldsmobile's trunk began to appear on the roads.

Not all of the downsizing and change was good - I thought of diet sodas and Yugos, but inventions like self-adhesive stamps and TV remote controls created an acceptable balance.

Bella was in the kitchen warming some water for the hot toddies, a night-cap and general cure-all passed down from long forgotten relatives along the shore. It was almost midnight when Bella brought the steaming concoction of hot lemon water, honey, and whisky into the living room, where I was occupying myself with a several decade old issue of Popular Mechanics. This magazine, like National Geographic, somehow never got thrown away. There were some interesting stories about the future of automobiles and flying wings that the Army was secretly developing, and I had to admire their bold predictions that were pretty close to what had actually been developed. Bella handed me the steaming toddy and sat next to me on the sofa, her legs folded gracefully beneath her. She appeared soft and lovely, despite the cold walk and the lateness of the hour.

I blew on my drink and was able to ingest a few small sips without scalding my lips or choking on the healthy amount of alcohol. The radiator clanged in the corner; its chipped blue painted surface emitting an almost visible heat.

I wondered whether or not the paint was lead-based. Bella was letting her drink cool a bit while warming her hands on the ceramic cup with a rose print and a small hairline crack that didn't quite go through to its contents. The wind outside howled as it blew strongly through the trees surrounding the cottage. Most of the leaves had already fallen and the empty branches made whip-like sounds that gave the night a life of its own. I had always found the wind eerie as a child, but at this stage in my life the sound was almost comforting.

Bella sipped her toddy, the whisky hitting the back of her throat, causing her to cough slightly. "Gets me every time," she said, an impish look of child-like fun animating her face. "I always get silly when I drink."

We both smiled. I looked at my cousin and asked her if she remembered Noni's jug of red wine that she used to keep under her bed, upstairs.

"The one for medicinal reasons?" Bella said with a smile.

"That's the one," I said, joining the mirth of our collective memories. "She always took a few 'medicinal' swigs before she went to bed at night. I remember when we were about ten or eleven, sneaking upstairs for a drink, filing the jug with water up to the line the wine had been at."

"I remember. I also seem to remember one of us catching a good whack from her when she noticed how diluted the jug had become." There was a twinkle in her eye.

"I seem to remember you getting me into a lot of trouble when we were kids." I said.

"Me?" Bella feigned righteous indignation. "I'm not the one who cut his finger off with Nono's home-made table saw and then try to duct tape it back on!"

This brought back a painful yet hysterical image of myself as a young boy and his favorite cousin on hands and knees looking for a severed appendage amidst the sawdust and tools in a dimly lit cellar. We were both hysterical, more scared about what Nono would do when he found out we used his power tools than worried about the fact that I'd never have full mobility of the finger.

I automatically looked at the fifth digit of my right hand and could, even after all these years, make out the few traces of the Doctor's stitches. "Another happy memory from youth," I groaned, exhaling deeply.

Bella started giggling.

"What?"

"The best one was you, Jimmy Carmichael, and the hammer."

"What's this morbid fascination you have with my injuries?" I smiled back.

"Well," Bella started, "technically it was Jimmy's injury, and it was pretty darn funny after we found out he'd be okay..."

I gave her a sly look, "What's in that drink of yours, Bella?"

Bella laughed hard. Jimmy Carmichael and I had been begging our fathers to let us build a tree fort in his backyard overlooking the pond in the park. We were about ten or eleven at the time, the summer before Tina died. Aunt Josie was watching us at the cottage, so Bella and I made a beeline for Jimmy's house just as soon as our parents left for the day to Mystic Seaport. Theresa was at the library and the younger cousins were hanging around the cottage trying to help Aunt Josie prepare lunch, but more often than not, getting in her way.

Bella and I took a couple of shortcuts up and over fences in our neighbor's yards, racing to Jimmy's. She beat me there, as always, and was catching her breath as I reached the finish line of the Carmichael driveway. Mr. Carmichael, a very imposing and distant sort of man was on his way into town for the entire afternoon. Mrs. Carmichael was away at her sister's house in Manchester, so Mr. Carmichael had hired the sitting service of a local girl home for the summer from the University in Storrs.

Knowing our intentions, and knowing how utterly irresponsible three pre-teens could be, Mr. Carmichael positively forbid us from making a tree fort while he was gone and was very precise with what punishments would be doled out if there was any tree-climbing done while the sitter (I think her name was Caroline) was in charge. He then took special pains to warn young Jimmy to stay away from his toolbox or be beaten like he'd never been beat before. These were the days when a smack on the head or a belt on the rear end was considered typical child-raising. The three of us agreed, of course, and I distinctly remember the look of apprehension on Mr. Carmichael's face as he pulled out of the driveway in his huge blue Chevy. We stood at the end of the driveway, our three cherub-like faces smiling ear to ear, and with extra reassurance we told him to enjoy the day and not to worry one bit. We even waved to him as he drove towards town.

The three of us watched Mr. Carmichael pull away from the house and turn right. We stood at the end of the driveway for a good five minutes, just in case he decided to circle around the block. Realizing he was gone for the day; we began foolishly laughing as we darted to his toolbox. Jimmy and I grabbed hammer, saw, and nails while Bella grabbed some screwdrivers and a level. With eyes constantly on the lookout for the sitter, we hurried around back and ran into the woods.

We had already picked out the perfect tree for our fort, and over the past few weeks had been accumulating a large cache of two-by-fours, plywood, and whatever other pieces of lumber we could get our hands on. We had piled the wood at the base of our chosen tree and had already tied ropes to the branches that were to be used in the hoisting of the wood into the tree. I was the first one to shimmy up the tree, finding the right footholds for the other two conspirators to follow. Reaching the well-hidden middle, I comfortably sat looking down at Bella and Jimmy Carmichael: "This is it!"

Bella was next up, finding another branch even with mine about six feet away. Jimmy Carmichael began by handing us a couple of strong boards for the platform, which we wedged between the thick branches. It was as if the tree had been made for this fort, so perfect did the boards fit, and we began to feel the satisfaction a sculptor feels when he removes the statue from inside the marble; it had not always been there, it just needed to come out. The weather was hot, the work was fun, and we knew that Mr. Carmichael would not be back for hours.

I slid down the tree and helped Jimmy hand Bella the planks we had acquired from some neighbor's fence that was being replaced. Bella laid them out, side by side, across the two-by-fours, forming the perfect base for our home away from home. Jimmy grabbed his dad's claw hammer, stuck it through his belt loops, put a couple dozen 16 penny nails in his pocket and climbed aboard. Kneeling like a professional carpenter, Jimmy Carmichael began nailing the planks to the two-by-fours, leaving as little space between them as possible. Our fort's floor couldn't hold water, but we didn't want to fall out of the tree due to shoddy workmanship.

We were having a great time together, partially because of the beautiful day around us; partially due to the act of civil disobedience we were taking part in with a vengeance. Jimmy Carmichael was hammering away, his swings becoming more fixed and more intense as he became more comfortable with the heavy hammer. When he got to the part where the two-by-four was propped into the tree, he decided that we had enough nails to use a few extra in securing the lumber to the tree itself and began hammering through the thick wood into the even thicker tree branch.

Each stroke of the hammer became an effort, and Jimmy Carmichael's young muscles fought with the difficulty of the task. I have always credited Bella for getting Jimmy Carmichael in this zone of productivity.

To give himself a better swing, Jimmy Carmichael grabbed the hammer with both hands and pounded the nail that was trying to bite the wood. Up went the hammer, down went the hammer. Up went the hammer, down went the hammer. Up went the hammer...."AAAAAGGGHHHH!" Jimmy Carmichael yelled as he held the hammer above his head. Bella and I looked at him smartly, waiting for the punch line of a laugh. None followed – the hammer's claw was imbedded in his skull, blood quickly matting his brown hair.

"AAAAGGHHHHH!", Jimmy Carmichael yelled again.

"AAAAGGHHHHH!", yelled Bella.

"AAAAGGHHHHH!", I yelled too.

Jimmy Carmichael was able to slide down the tree, unable or unwilling to pull the claw end of the hammer from his head. The three of us stood looking quite pale for a couple of long seconds, then Bella grabbed his arm and quickly led us to the back door of his house. The sitter greeted us at the door with a look of wonder on her face that quickly disappeared as the reality of the situation came into her mind.

"AAAAAGGGGHHH!", she yelled.

"AAAAAGGGGHHH", Jimmy Carmichael yelled back at her.

Bella and I decided it was a good time to make a speedy exit and ran back to the cottage. Jimmy Carmichael ended up being okay, the blood was just from cut skin, and the hammer did not puncture the skull. I don't think I'll ever forget the look on the face of the sitter, who, after this episode, refused all work from the Carmichael and my family.

I also will never forget the whipping I received from Nono after Mr. Carmichael came to the cottage and explained that his son was in Hartford Hospital due to our blatant disobedience regarding the use of his tools. Most of their conversation was in loud Italian (is there any other?), and as soon as I saw Nono's hand go for his belt I knew that I was in for it. Usually, with bad behavior, the offending party just had to outrun the other cousins and not get caught, but this was one time when I was clearly in his sights.

Bella was smiling; no doubt she had just relived the Jimmy Carmichael story as well. "Good times," she said lifting her glass in a mock toast to mine. I returned her toast with a roll of the eyes and a quick smile. "Good times," I said.

16.

The cottage had warmed up nicely, and the whisky in the hot toddy was relaxing me into a sleep I was trying desperately to fight – I wanted to enjoy Bella's company uninterrupted for as long as possible.

"Does Mary ever get out your way?", I asked, referring to Bella's younger sister.

"Occasionally," she offered. "With Leo's job she does a lot of traveling around and hosting get-togethers. Sometimes I get a little jealous of all the places she's been – she even spent a year in Hawaii. Me, I've never left New England, except to see you and Susan in Florida. I think it must be hard on Leo Junior and Tracy too, especially having to change schools so often." Bella became reflective, "Leo Junior's been in some trouble, too. Kids that move around a lot tend to fall in with the wrong crowd. They don't have time to sort out who the good ones are, and a little trouble makes them feel special. I wouldn't want to try to raise Alex away from his family and friends."

I thought about this for a moment or two, finished my drink and said, "I always have thought that Mary likes it though. She always talked about traveling, reading those romance novels late into the night whenever she was here at the cottage. I think that's why she enjoys being a nurse; she can find a job anywhere."

The cold glass windows framed in wood behind the sofa vibrated softly as a gust of wind blew in more cold weather from lands even further north. Bella's eyes were beginning to close. "About ready to turn in?", I asked her, a part of me wishing her to say no, a part of me wanting her to get a good night's rest so we could continue on in the morning refreshed and relaxed.

"It's late," Bella said. She rose in a simple graceful manner, took my cup, and walked into the kitchen. My eyes followed her small form, ever marveling at the ease in which she moved herself. I stood and checked the door and the temperature of the heater, straightened the pillows on the sofa, and turned off the living room light. Bella had turned off the kitchen lights, and was standing next to me, a dreamy smile on her face.

"I could sleep for a week," she said. "The ocean air always gets to me." Bella yawned and stretched her arms, her loose sweatshirt falling over her body. I put my arms around her waist and gently pulled her into an embrace.

"I'm glad you're here," I said hugging her, our faces only inches apart. The closer one got to

Bella, the more easily one could appreciate her beauty. She smiled.

"I knew you'd want me here," she said, returning my hug by tightening her arms around my shoulders. We said good night, and I walked her upstairs to the entrance of Noni's old room, oblivious to the creaking stairs or any other external noises, so wrapped up in the moment that nothing else existed.

"Night," Bella smiled, leaning up and kissing my cheek before entering the room that was to be hers tonight. I momentarily stood at the closed door, then turned to the left and went into the room I had set up in. I put on a pair of sweats and kept on my thick socks. Even though I had turned the heat up a bit, there were only vents in Noni's room and my bedroom faced north. It was always colder than the rest of the house, and Susan wasn't with me on this trip for bodily warmth.

I took a Xanax to help me sleep – another sign of age and my refusal to accept the natural body rhythms associated with this stage of my life. I left the light on and climbed into bed, the firm mattress not yielding to my body weight due to the piece of plywood Uncle Frankie had put between the mattress and box spring. A small but persistent draft entered through the window above me, sending a shiver down my spine. I opened my worn copy of St. Augustine's City of God and began reading some favorite passages.

I'm not sure if it was the hour or because I was so familiar with this work, but I had a difficult time concentrating on the words staring up from the highlighted dog-eared pages. I closed my eyes and realized it was neither hour nor content; it was Bella. She was in my mind now more than ever, her proximity felt so deeply in my heart that it almost hurt. I tried to read it again. I turned and looked at the wall separating the two of us. I made a physical effort to turn away and tried to concentrate.

Hundreds of images filled my mind of Bella and the cottage. We were kids again, racing to the shore. Playing ball with Jimmy Carmichael. We were ice skating and sneaking cigarettes. Swimming and eating pizza. We were holding hands on the jetty and getting ready for school. Bella and I were dancing together at a school formal one moment and telling ghost stories to scare Elizabeth and the twins the next. We were laughing as the first flakes of winter glided down as beautiful crystals from heaven. We were climbing trees and crying at Tina's funeral, eating freshly made gnocchi and squeezing vine-ripened tomatoes for a sauce.

Moments later, we were young adults double-dating and packing me off to go to college.

We were driving into New York together to spend the weekend in Little Italy or taking a day trip into the North End of Boston. Bella was helping me study for exams Saturdays at the Hartford library. We were eating Sicilian pizza together for dinner and toasting each other on New Year's Eve.

Time moved forward as my thoughts raced ahead. Bella was getting married to Jimmy; Bella was having Alex. I married Susan and moved to Florida while Bella divorced Jimmy and stayed at the cottage. Time moved on and Susan gave birth to Antony and Bella married Michael. Time moved on and we visited each other whenever we could, taking our families to Disney one year and Washington D.C. the next. We saw each other at funerals and weddings as the visits became logistically impossible to plan. We still managed to talk at 7pm each Sunday night.

Along the way we experienced the gifts of fruitful marriages. Country fairs and family reunions, T-ball games, and proms. There were pulled teeth and new pets, trips to the mall and the unquenchable laughter of children's birthday parties. These things happened...we have pictures to prove it... but somehow things were different. We were growing up.

Life was everything all put together at one time, not a series of unrelated events, I thought as I turned the light off. Life was this, that, and everything else, all thrown at you, demanding a response. Every move I made, every decision I reached, always had some effect on someone, somewhere who would in turn somehow affect me, or someone else. From a skinned knee that caused Antony momentary pain, to the anguish of the first day Elizabeth started high school, life appeared at this late hour to be a series of events that were like a stone thrown into a calm lake producing various size waves and ripples, depending on how big the stone was; or with what velocity it was thrown. Some ripples made it to the shore, some died out before they completed their journey. I looked at my watch, it was after two a.m.

I thought about Bella and how much of my life she had shared with me, the continuous thread of stability and love. She had been there since the beginning when our parents put us in the same crib, and we recognized the fact that there was more to the world than Dad and Mom. She was there as the first steps were taken and we learned to talk within a week of each other. We crawled together, stood together, laughed together. We were more than friends, closer than cousins. We were inseparable as children and discovered a bond that would last a lifetime, growing closer as we aged.

We were always together when we could be, and no other person or situation could ever drive us apart. Our love for each other outlasted friends, lovers, even marriages. We were truly unique and that was truly wonderful; not only to experience such a relationship but to actually recognize it and see it for what it is. Each moment together was not only lived but was enjoyed.

It was 2:30. I knew that morning would come fast so I tried to slow down my thoughts in an effort to step into the realm of unconsciousness and sleep, if only for a few hours. Fifteen minutes later I was still wide awake and decided to go downstairs for a drink of cold water. I got up from the bed, put on my slippers and started out of the bedroom. As I passed Noni's old room, I gently pushed the door that was ajar, holding my breath, hoping the old metal hinges wouldn't creak. The warmth of the cottage had apparently warmed the metal surface and my exhaling ended up louder than the motion of the door.

I looked inside the room. Bella was asleep, her knees pulled up against her chest as she slept peacefully in the fetal position. The lightweight white blanket fell gently over her small frame as she faced the wall, her back toward the door where I stood. The rhythmic rising of her chest as she tranquilly breathed made me smile, and I inhaled her scent that filled the room.

If someone stares long enough at someone who is sleeping, something in the sleeping person somehow registers this information and their slumber is usually interrupted as they drift back into consciousness. As I stood watching Bella's peaceful repose, she realized I was there and rolled over slowly to look at me. "Hey," she said, her eyes not quite fully open, "you okay?"

"Just having a hard time falling asleep," I said, part of me disappointed in my having interrupted her dreams, part of me happy to hear her soft voice and see her so relaxed. "I'm sorry I woke you," I apologized. "I'm just going downstairs to get a drink of cold water."

"Bring me one up also," she replied, a smile that included that special sparkle of her eyes.

I smiled and walked down the old wooden stairs and went into the kitchen. I turned on the small single bulb set behind a gaslight-shaped glass etched with roses. The switch turned with a distinct 'click' and the pale-yellow light from the forty-watt bulb provided enough light to see without offending my sense of sight this late in the evening. I took two glasses from the cabinet over the sink as I ran the cool tap water, filling them each halfway. I fit the base of both in my left hand and walked out of the kitchen, turning off the glowing light.

As I passed through the living room, I noticed the condensation on the pane of glass that was immediately behind the radiator and wondered how cold it was outside. I now had a glass in each hand in an effort not to spill the ice-cold water on the hardwood floors. I walked over to the front door and squinted through the window. It was pitch black outside; the large trees and some clouds obscuring the light of the new moon and the stars overhead, but I could faintly make out the reading on the thermometer. Uncle Sal had hammered it onto the wall across from this window, underneath the light of the yellow bulb that let people know someone was living here. Twenty-eight degrees. I instinctively shivered – it was cold for this time of year.

I turned and went back up the stairs, creaking as each foot was placed in sequence on the assent to Noni's room. "Come in," Bella said softly.

"Still counting steps?" I said, referring to our childhood habit of knowing when someone was approaching our room – fifteen creaky steps.

"I was counting sheep until my favorite cousin woke me up to bring me water," she said with a distinct lightness in her voice.

I went into the room. Bella was sitting up against a pillow in the dark room, the only light a dim glow from the moon emerging from behind its cloud covering and a small tear-drop nightlight that had a glass montage of the Virgin Mary holding the Christ child.

A pair of Noni's old rosaries were draped as they had always been, over the bedpost. In the corner was the old ewer and wash basin, set on a mahogany table that matched the bedposts and the room's two dressers. Pictures of the family stood in shadow on the nightstand, and I could just barely make out my figure in the old oval stand-alone mirror in the far corner of the room next to an old rocking chair Uncle Gino had made for her.

Bella was now sitting upright on the bed, her back against a large white down pillow, gracefully propped up against the headboard. She had moved to the far side of the bed, and patting the unoccupied side closest to her said, "Come sit down."

I walked over to her, handed her one of the water glasses filled with the cold tap water, took a drink from mine, and sat down next to her. The warmth from the radiator vent could be felt easily in this room; I removed my slippers and propped my head up on my hand, my elbow resting on a fluffy pillow. Bella lifted her arm, and I rested my head in the calming silence. She stroked my hair as one would a child, reassuringly and in control, no complaints about being woken up during the middle of the night.

“I wish I could make this easier for you,” she said, her hand gently resting on my shoulder.

“You are,” I said, my eyelids tightly closing. I felt comforted. I could not, at this moment, imagine there being any other place in the entire world that I would rather be or anyone whom I would rather be with. The moment was tender, it was loving, it was a lifetime of trust and memories culminating in two people sitting side by side, uncertain of the future, but knowing they would somehow share it together. I began to doze, my waking and dreaming states becoming linked. I was awake and I was here at the cottage, I was asleep dreaming I was in the same place.

I barely heard the sound of the radiator or even the wind from off the ocean against the thin window glass. I was all at once here and nowhere, totally and completely yielding to the surroundings of the cottage and the tender embrace of Bella. I don’t remember falling asleep or when she stopped stroking my hair. I know she must have nodded off close to three a.m. because that’s when I stirred momentarily from my carefree slumber. For one last time I was not the decision maker; the one that had to stand up as a sentinel against life's everyday attacks. I was prone. I was the one being shielded and protected, the first time in oh so many years. Sleep came to me – rather it engulfed me – and no thoughts of life's petty intrusions could disturb such a complete sleep as this.

My mind floated. I soared above mountain tops, visited lush green valleys, and tasted the salt from the ocean's foam. I smelled the light fragrance of a violet bloom. I wasn't running anymore; not away from anything. Not towards anything. There, in the stillness of the cottage, I slept in an evening what seemed to be days, so lost was I in her care and my good fortune.

SUNDAY

1.

After a night of deep sleep, the smell of bacon frying awoke me from comforting dreams, and I turned over to face the clock. I realized that I had slept until almost nine o'clock, a luxury I had not allowed myself for many years. The sun was shining through the small bedroom windows, bathing me in a beautiful light. The light and my waking happy mood seemed to lift my spirit heavenwards, and I sat still for several minutes not wanting to move but live in this present moment.

Bella was of course downstairs, and I could hear her moving dishes and pans, preparing my breakfast. The breakfast would undoubtedly be four eggs fried in bacon grease, some black coffee made on the stove, and whatever fruit was the freshest at market that morning. I looked over to where she had slept last night, her slight impression still just visible on the bed spread. I stretched and yawned, breathing in deeply both the surrounding smell of breakfast and Bella's scent that still lingered in this small room. I've heard it said that people actually can rely on the sense of smell for a more accurate description of their surroundings than the sense of sight; more could be discerned from smells than from a quick visual glance. At this moment I believed this must be so – although I would take the loss of smell over the loss of sight without question.

I lifted my body out of the warm bed, hearing just audible creaks in the floor, and also in my joints, a reminder that I was no longer twenty. The floor had always had the creaks, my body seemed to gain more every day. The hum of the radiator still going told me that the cold weather of last night had decided to stick around a bit longer, despite the brilliant sunshine entering the bedroom. I stretched to the floor a few times to work out the stiffness in my back and went downstairs carrying a pair of socks and running shoes that I had taken from the bedroom that had allowed me to sleep the night before.

Bella greeted me at the stair's landing with a cheerful "good morning" and a soft kiss on the cheek. I was acutely aware that I needed to brush my teeth and wash up before having any sort of social interaction, so I smiled sheepishly and said "hey there" as I headed into the bathroom, Bella's slight laughter at my personal vanity followed close behind.

"You slept well," I heard her say over the running water that I was washing my face in.

"Did I snore?"

Bella laughed, "And then some! When was the last time you got a decent night's sleep?"

"What year is this?" I jokingly responded, the toothbrush in my mouth muffling the clarity of my enunciation.

"You made up for it last night anyway," she called to me. "I've got bacon and eggs here after you get back from your jog...the melon's a little firm but it's still sweet."

I loved the way Bella knew my routine. A morning run had been a part of my everyday health program since high school and had continued through my adult years. I used to joke that my running kept me sane, but there is probably some truth to it. While Bella and I were living together before I married Susan and she found Michael, she had joined me most days and then cooked a breakfast that I'm sure almost negated any health benefits the exercising afforded.

I came out of the bathroom feeling much more human and walked up behind my cousin as she stood slicing a honeydew melon into bite-sized squares in the kitchen sink, icy tap water running softly. "Morning," I said as she smiled over her shoulder at me.

"You look much better now," Bella said hugging me around the neck with hands slightly dripping water and melon juice onto the back of my shirt.

"Thank you for last night," I said with total conviction and sincerity as our embrace parted. "I really have needed you. I've got a lot going on up here and I had a thousand thoughts running through my mind. I really needed the sleep I got."

I stepped back a bit, feeling slightly selfish, "I hope I didn't keep you up too long," I said.

Bella smiled. "You did, but it's ok. You kind of get used to sleepless nights when you have kids, and I was happy that we had some time together again. I watched you sleep until I finally nodded off."

"You tired now?" I asked.

"A little. I'll take a nap later though." She kissed me on my cheek. "Get going. Enjoy your jog, but hurry back, I'm starving." And with that said, she turned smartly to the sink and continued dicing the melon.

I reached around her and grabbed a piece of honeydew, "just one," I said as I headed to the front door. I turned the knob and walked outside, immediately assaulted by an arctic blast of icy breeze, its intensity magnified by its sheer force. It really *was* windy. And cold. I momentarily debated whether or not I should goback inside the cottage and grab a sweatshirt but decided that the best thing to do was just to keep moving and move quickly.

I started out heading in the same direction Bella and I traveled last night, away from the impending construction of the Branford Beautification Project. I wanted to enjoy my run without distraction from anything negative. I consciously determined that seeing anything remotely associated with the destruction of what I had experienced again last night would cast shadows on this beautiful day I knew in my heart I could fully enjoy.

I began at a slow warm-up pace, the rhythm of my shoes hitting pavement gradually increasing in speed as my blood began to circulate throughout my cold body. It was another beautiful day at the shore, less congested this early on a Sunday morning. Church hadn't started yet, and it was a good ten degrees cooler than last night, despite the brightly shining sun. Few cars passed me as I ran along the gravel shoulder, lost in thought yet keeping aware of the uneven terrain. The memory of a bad fall and sprain along this road years ago still made me slightly cringe as well as reminding me why I was never able to play professional sports.

The sun was higher in the sky today than when I had set out yesterday morning, and despite the cool temperature, rays of heat from the sun coursed through my body. No clouds were obstructing the warmth and a sense of calmness washed over me. Only a couple of cars had been parked at the beach, most likely belonging to the very old or the very young. The youngsters squeeze out one final day at the shore now that winter winds were blowing in; the elderly coming to sit in silent revelry, marveling at the beauty of God's creation.

Seagulls could be heard in the distance, each trying desperately to forage enough food for the day and store some as body fat in case tomorrow's hunting was not as profitable. I had always found it amazingly ironic that as the weather got colder and the food supply decreased, the need for food increased, causing what could have been taken as riotous cries from the desperate birds. If one were to ascribe human characteristics to the lesser beings on this planet, the gulls would be having a free-for-all to wrestle away whatever food they could from their neighbor who was trying to overstuff himself before anyone noticed. I now began to mentally compare the frantic spasms of the seabirds to the almost calmness of the bear that slowly, throughout the year builds up enough fat and body weight to be almost unaffected by the time winter finally would show up, gladly sleeping through the cold months only to wake eventually well-rested and quite a bit thinner.

I tripped on a small rock, caught myself, and wondered how I could have gotten so absorbed in random thoughts of birds and bears that really had no effect on my life. I chided myself silently, remembering how as a student I had cursed the writings of Melville and Hemingway for their digressions into the most mundane of thoughts. Shaking off the slight pain in my left ankle, I determined that life was sometimes like that – a bunch of detours that brought you to a climax you never would have expected.

As I continued my jog, I wondered about the many directions my life could have taken and what the outcomes could have been. Had I not broken my left ankle that summer, would I still be a psychiatrist or perhaps a baseball player? Had Tina survived the fall through the ice – what changes would she have brought to her family? Without the cottage in my early life, would Bella and I be so very close, and was I somehow robbing my children of the opportunity to share life's wonders with their extended family members by selling the cottage? Or, was keeping the cottage the wrong choice to make – perhaps money that would be distributed to each family member would be used in a special way that would affect their lives more than the cottage would? I often wondered if when we die God allows us to see what our lives should have been compared what they were. Then, He'd tell us how close or far we were from the path that would have been best.

A blue Toyota drove past me at about thirty miles an hour, the driver giving me a friendly 'toot' on the horn as I began to slow down to a more comfortable and longer-lasting pace. I smiled instinctively although I knew the gesture would not have been noticed in a rearview mirror as the car continued around the bend heading toward the ball field. I wondered what gestures would go unnoticed as the bulldozers were plowing down the cottage. Did it matter that I was in such mental duress? Aside from Bella and Theresa, did anyone really care that my sleep was being interrupted and my mind filled with clutter? Or were my actions as unknown as my smile was to the driver of that car heading around another curve hitting bumps along the way that only stayed with him for a brief moment?

I slowed again to a walking pace as my ankle began to register pain. I was determined to just enjoy this moment in time and stop letting my mind wander. When I reached the ballfield, I ran the bases and headed back to the cottage where I knew, with great expectation, that in addition to a wonderful breakfast, I would shortly be enjoying Bella's company again. The cold air stung my exposed arms despite the now fully risen sun, and I picked up my pace as I eagerly headed home.

Home. That's what it was, and that sentiment is what I felt was missing from the family members who wanted me to sell. This burden I was shouldering was an attempt to destroy what I identified as my home. Whenever I thought of going back home, it was always here, despite the years I had lived in Florida, and despite the fact that I never lived at the cottage. My family had always lived in Hartford, but home was here in Branford. I was frustrated that other family members had chosen to call the cottage simply a vacation home, when in reality it was the place where our childish dreams turned into adult memories.

I would spend nine months a year going to school and coming home to the uncertainties all youth must face, but I'd spend every other weekend at the shore. Then, as if some Divine Decree had been sent down from Heaven above, summer vacation would start, and the cottage would become my true home. I identified with and loved the family that would be there, and I had life-long friends to share my juvenile adventures with. And it was here that Bella and I would always meet, months of separation turning into a blur as we renewed our friendship and love within moments of arrival.

The blast from the green Mustang wasn't as friendly as the toot I received earlier as I apparently drifted a little too close to the traffic that was picking up along the beach road. I needed to get back before I let my wandering mind drift me into a moving vehicle. With an act of concentration, I finished the last quarter mile, and walked up the gravel path to the cottage with my hands on my hips and steam coming from my mouth with each exhale. I did a couple of cool-down squats, stretched a bit, and headed inside. The door was, of course, unlocked and the smell of fried eggs and bacon drew me into the kitchen.

2.

"Smells wonderful," I offered up as I saw Bella wiping down the kitchen counter with a yellow sponge.

"Just waiting for you," she said with a smile on her face and in her voice. "You want to shower first? The food will keep."

And I knew it would, as I said, "I'll just be about a minute or so." Food always seemed to keep here at the cottage. I don't remember *not* having food out somewhere, but I do remember that no one seemed to ever get sick from it. One would think that with all the preservatives and additives in today's foods that they would be immune from the dangers doctors and journalists led us to believe.

I went into the bathroom, shut the door, and turned the shower on hot. Steam quickly filled the small room as I dropped my clothes and entered the stall. The warm water flooded my skin, and I felt as though it was actually entering my bones; the warmth pulling the brittle cold from this morning's jog out of my body. My flesh was becoming pink, and I knew Bella was waiting for me to come eat breakfast, although she would never think of rushing me or seem impatient.

Cognizant of this, I lathered and rinsed, then stepped out shutting the shower off. I dried quickly, the bathmat a pleasant cushion to my feet as I avoided stepping on what I knew to be a cold terrazzo floor.

I put on the pair of blue jeans and a white T-shirt that Bella had laid out for me, slipped on a pair of wool socks, and gelled my hair. Bella was serving our breakfast as I exited the only bathroom which happened to be adjacent to the small kitchen, a trail of steam like a shadow. She had put eggs, bacon, and toast on both our plates, and had arranged the cubed melon and some cheese on two small plates just within reach. I sat down at the table with Bella on my left and after saying a brief prayer, began to eat heartily.

"You must have gotten up early," I said, holding a piece of toast to my mouth.

Bella: "I was up around seven. I drove into town – you wouldn't believe the size of the grocery store."

"I was in there yesterday. You could drop at least five of the old stores inside it." I said, drinking some room temperature black coffee.

"I kind of miss the old one," she said, "but this one is so convenient. It had already been open for an hour before I got there. On a Sunday even."

The old food mart had always been closed on the Lord's Sabbath, whereas the shareholders of this new mega store wanted the collection plate passed around their store seven days a week. I served Bella some melon and took up a few pieces for myself. She was right – it was sweet but too firm to be considered ripe, another sign that the local produce farmer had been unceremoniously replaced by some produce megalith out of California or Mexico that picked the fruit before it was ready. For that matter, all of the apples were now the same size and polished with a sealing wax to lock in the unnaturally bright colors. A Brave New World of produce had come to this quiet town.

"I talked with Susan this morning," Bella said while daintily nibbling a piece of dry toast. "She was glad I was here to take care of you. Antony is OK and she said she missed you."

"You're the one that's here for me, Bella," I said.

She thought about this for a moment as she ate a bit of melon.

"Susan *loves* you," Bella finally managed. "She may not understand you the way I do, but she really does care."

"I know. But after the passion started turning into years of complacency, I really wish we were stronger together – like you and Michael."

"Or you and me," she smiled.

"That too," I replied.

We sat in silence for a good five minutes, each of us lost in our thoughts regarding the proper amount of love a marriage should have. Sure, Susan and I trusted each other, cared for each other's feelings, enjoyed each other on the occasions when our two bodies were in the throes of passion, and generally were concerned with each other's welfare. But was that enough? Was that the extent of the human condition known as love? But having once – and continuously – tasted being totally enraptured by the very soul of a person, was I deluding myself in thinking that any relationship could possibly provide as much fulfillment on so many different levels of being? In short, was Susan the best and wisest choice I could have made in this mortal shell under the constraints of family, the Church, and society as a whole? Was the complete and total love I felt with Bella able to be had in another person? And if it could be, was Susan the person that this totality was to be found with, or had I wasted a decade of my life somehow settling for comfortable complacency in a mediocre relationship? These were my thoughts as I watched my cousin delicately finish a piece of cubed cheese.

She must have sensed my deep concentration and soulful introspection, for out of the blue she said in an authoritative tone, "Give me your jacket buddy!", a twinkle in her blue eyes.

I laughed automatically, immediately being snapped from the clutches of introspection. Bella had somehow chosen a reference to our sortie into downtown Boston during my first year at the University. We had decided to drive up and spend the day in Beantown over twenty years ago, when ChinaTown was called the "Combat Zone" and years before the Big Dig. The weather was cold, not simply crisp, and my grandfather had lent me his knee-length tweed London Fog coat he had purchased with much pride at G. Fox & Co., when their only competition was Montgomery Ward in downtown Hartford. Both companies have since exited the marketplace, as the Wal-Martification of America has changed the way in which we now shop. Woolworth and Woolco, two other downtown staples, have also closed their doors after being in business for the better part of a century.

Bella and I were young then, and as typical youth we were so very excited about our plans for the day. We got up early, inhaled a quick breakfast, and were on our way for the two-and-a-half-hour trip into Boston. We filled the car with our plans for not just this day, but of dreams of the future, dreams only partially realized or long forgotten on this side of memory.

We found a place to park near Boylston Street, walked past the swan boats and headed to Faneuil Hall. We spent the day in the open-air market, haggling over prices and eating a delicious bowl of lobster bisque for lunch. I remember buying a couple of egg cream sodas from an outdoor vendor; we simply enjoyed each other's company. We ate and drank with gusto, saw ducks emerge from a ritzy hotel, sat in the park and people-watched for a while. Around dinner time, Bella and I purposely avoided the touristy places like Cheers and walked hand in hand into the North End of Boston, where English was the second language to the Italian merchants, and we felt right at home. It was wonderful - the delicious smells of freshly cooked meals and breads, surrounded by conversations that we were semi-privy to, our Italian being not as fluent as our parents.

We ate homemade pasta at a little place called Maria's, had a couple glasses of Sangria (the drinking age was eighteen then), and enjoyed spumoni and cannoli made with fresh cheese and a side of fruit. The weather had grown bitterly cold as the sun set and I was thankful for my grandfather's tweed coat as we prepared to leave. I put on my leather gloves and turned up the collar of the coat as we left Maria's, Bella's arm wrapped tenderly around mine. She was dressed to the nines, her youthful beauty causing men of all ages to ignore their own partners for as much time as it took to stop and stare.

A feeling of pride mixed with vanity overtook my senses and I was warm from the wine and Bella's closeness. Being very young, and with this youth being very adventurous, decisions sometimes are made that seem wonderful at the time but looked back upon as rash or foolhardy. Such was the case for Bella and me, entering the subway heading for the above-mentioned Combat Zone at nine o'clock at night.

Lost in our own thoughts and each other's conversation, we were oblivious to the ever-changing and increasingly menacing reprobates that were entering at each stop. Chinatown during the mid-eighties was a literal den of inequity, packed with people from all walks of the underbelly of society. Here they all were – the drunks, vomiting on the sidewalk; the hookers, trying to peddle their wares; the junkies shooting up on the subway's terminal steps... and beautiful Bella, a shocked look upon her face. Sure, during the day you could still buy a live chicken for dinner at any number of the small temporary booths, but here at night, we were two people definitely in the wrong place.

But, as I mentioned before, we were young and adventurous with a giddy feeling of false security penetrating our hearts and minds as we stepped off the underground train at the Chinatown station – along with a small contingency of partygoers, junkies, and other banal pleasure-seekers. I instinctively held Bella close as we stepped off the platform and over a drunk who was in the process of losing what little supper was in his stomach. There were a few cat-calls and offers made to each of us or both as we ascended the concrete stairs into the Red-Light District of Boston's dark side, trying hard at not guessing what it was that was making our shoes stick to the ground.

Upon reaching the platform, Bella and I paused a moment, the sights and sounds of blended languages and races rivaled only by New York City. Large paper lanterns of various colors and states of disarray hung unceremoniously from lamp stands that supported the weight of the usual drunks and working girls, some who could not have been older than Bella herself. Splashes of neon signs were everywhere, reds and yellows, greens and oranges, all illuminating the evening with their artificial glare, adding to the surreal feeling of Chinatown. We walked along one of the numbered streets, approached by various people for various reasons. Some requests were nothing more than loose change or a cigarette. The more offensive ones boldly suggested some sort of Bacchus revelry that included Bella and me and perhaps some alcohol.

Despite the late hour, street vendors shouted out prices to passersby's, more often than not in a broken English with a Bostonian accent. Fresh fish were being bathed in ice, egg rolls were being deep fried, and Sake was being served in a corner café that promoted its famous steam room. Large billboards announced the latest in drinking tonics with orange or red Chinese characters and smiling geishas, while decrepit marquis touted English dubbed films showing every forty minutes or so, usually three large red X's following the title.

And wall to wall people. The number of souls held captive in this strange Babylon by choice or fate was staggering. It seemed that one could not move five feet without in some way coming into physical contact with another person who was totally removed from your life. Amidst this crush of humanity whose background was illuminated by neon glows, Bella and I forged on, stopping a moment here to look at novelty jewelry and a moment there to wait for the crowd to move ahead of us. There seemed to be no vehicles on the road as the mass of people flowed freely from sidewalk to road to restaurant and back again. With all the noise and claustrophobic feeling, I wasn't surprised to find Bella tugging on my arm, trying to direct me to a less-traveled alleyway as a possible escape from all this human madness.

I followed Bella's lead, and as a slight rain began to fall, we ducked down any alleyway off 8th Street and under the steel grates of apartments that should have been condemned years ago but were apparently still occupied. Bella was laughing and out of breath, her red cheeks and blue eyes showing her obvious pleasure at where our detour had led us. Despite the revelry and absurdity of Chinatown, it was an adventure, and Bella's innocent laughter joined with mine as I swung her around a couple of times.

"Fantastic!", she gasped, her white teeth and soft features visible in the glare of a solitary lamppost. Somewhere overhead the background noise of an old TV melded with an incessant mewing of a stray cat apparently in heat. "Just fantastic!", she smiled again. We were breathless with excitement, the sights and sounds of the big city combining with the ever-lurking aspect of potential danger speeding adrenaline into our veins. As the rain began to turn to sleet, we reflected on the plight of this unknown society, the sadness of the junkies, and which lady of the evening was truly a woman.

As we stood laughing gaily and talking about the flood of people that somehow lived here, we both became aware of someone approaching us at a reasonable, yet deliberate pace. The shadowy figure took shape into that of a man, long hair that appeared sticky and unkempt, a two-to-three-day growth of beard upon his weathered face and his right hand tucked into his faded and ripped blue jeans. As this stranger approached us, we began to notice his mannerisms. Eyes darting from Bella to the street, a definite tick on the right side of his face, and a look of controlled uneasiness settling across his features as he quickly drew near.

He stopped about five feet in front of us, and we noticed he was probably in his late twenties, the time that one is neither young nor old. The man's visible hand was shaking slightly, his eyes still darting back and forth between Bella and myself. "Nice jacket," he said, his voice beginning to crack. "Real nice jacket-it's cold out here...that's a fine jacket." His words came quickly and in snappy semi-sentences. "It sure is cold out here...and that jacket looks warm."

Bella and I had naturally begun walking away from him towards the quickly thinning crowd of Chinatown's icy streets. The man approached us more directly and began motioning with his hand that was inside his shirt, implying that there was more in his shirt than just his hand. He then stepped smartly in front of me and in a stern voice got down to the matter at hand. “Nice coat. Take it off. Quick. Nice coat. Give me it now.”

I must pause here to remind myself again that Bella and I were young at the time, and youth naturally lends itself to a feeling of invincibleness. In retrospect, with the hindsight of age and some wisdom, I can with great confidence say that first of all we would not have been in that alley in that section of town at that time of night, and most certainly my response to a crazed man that appeared to have a weapon under his shirt would have been much different.

But I had not learned yet that bravado and indignation can lead to personal injury, and besides, it was my grandfather’s coat, and I couldn’t back down in front of Bella. I looked at the stranger, who by this time was rocking back and forth while almost convulsively shaking, noticed that he was only a couple of inches taller than I was, so I made up my mind that the next coat he had was not going to be mine.

The stranger in an increasingly angry voice, “I SAID give me the coat!”

“Well,” I began as smoothly as I could, hoping my speech was not trembling too much. “I’ll tell you what. If you pull your hand out of your shirt and it's just your hand, I'm gonna smack you in the head. If there is only a knife, we'll see who's stronger. If you pull out a gun...then you can have my coat, no questions asked."

It took a moment or two as we watched him try to figure out where he lost the upper hand, and why this mugging wasn't going the way he planned. You could tell that he just couldn't wrap his brain around this one. "But I want your coat...", he finally stammered.

"Me too," I said, growing slightly bolder with each passing moment. I continued, "It's my grandfather's coat and there is really just no way I'm giving it up without seeing a gun." Realizing that we were probably no longer in any danger of being shot, I launched into righteous indignation.

"Last chance. Either pull out a gun or hit the road." I stood firm and held my ground.

The man looked at me with a perplexed bewilderment, apparently not being used to this sort of circumstance. In anger, and apparent disgust, he took out his empty hand, hit himself on the leg, exclaimed "Man...this sucks," and then absently turned around on his heel and stormed away, becoming an immediate focal point of brevity to us, and eventually as the years passed, became quite a fun story to tell at get-togethers.

Bella came over to me as she had done that night. "My hero," she smiled as I leaned back in the chair with my coffee, a smile still on my face all these years later.

"Well, I couldn't have let him have my coat," I said with mock sternness.

"That was the funniest thing," Bella said, putting some butter on a piece of toast. "You are aware that you totally ruined that man's self-esteem that night. I bet all the other robbers in Boston still make fun of him."

"Just desserts", I said. "Approaching two helpless teenagers like that."

Bella's eyes sparkled, "You may have been many things in your life, but helpless? Not so much."

"Yeah, I was lucky. That whole scene could have had a very different ending if he was really carrying a gun."

Bella smiled and bit into the now-buttered toast. I continued, "I really don't know what got into me. I was shaking from head to toe, scared out of my wits, but there was no way I was coming back here without that coat."

Bella took a drink of coffee. "I always thought you were just trying to impress me," she said half-jokingly.

"Well of course," I said, smiling. "But you have to admit that was one fine coat."

"That you ended up giving to one of your girlfriends if I remember correctly..."

I twitched. “Yeah, like I said, youth is filled with bad decisions. I think it was Joy who ended up with it. She was living in Jersey at the time.”

“You should have kept the coat and got rid of her,” Bella reminded me.

“Meow,” I said laughing.

Bella looked at me, “I’m just saying that Joy wasn’t one of your better moves.”

I smiled at my cousin. “Madam are you in some way suggesting that as a youth I could be persuaded to go out with a girl and give her the coat that was my grandfather’s.... especially after the night we had in Boston?”

“Not only am I suggesting it sir, but I am implying that the members of the fairer sex have always been able to have such a sway as to receive certain gifts and favors from you, even if they in no way deserved such gifts and favors.”

“I’m appalled,” I returned, “such members of the fairer sex have little or no sway....,” I broke off as Bella was laughing quite plainly at the frequency in which I had found myself attached to many young women and the gifts I had showered upon them, most of which were undeserving.

“Joy was quite a piece of work,” Bella managed to say while still laughing, “I never really got you and her.”

“She had certain attributes...,” I ventured.

"Ah, but a fair smile and physical perfection do not a person make."

"To a twenty-year-old guy that's pretty important, though I did see her a few years ago. Age had not been kind to the fair Joy. It must be difficult to grow older when style always triumphed over substance."

3.

Bella smiled at me, one of those sweet smiles common to springtime, but few and far between in winter, when they become much more appreciated. We were both done with breakfast, Bella had poured each of us more coffee, and I began to put aside the used plates as one puts aside childish things and returned from thoughts of Joy to the serious business at hand and thoughts of a new day at the cottage. My feelings of deep conviction toward my cousin must have been plainly scripted across my face as Bella began a simple yet demanding line of questioning. Or perhaps she just knew me so well that she knew what I needed to hear and what I needed to say.

"There's that look again Vincent," she started.

"Which one is that fair Bella?" exhaling slightly as I tried to have some degree of composure guide my speech and appearance. Whenever we began talking about other women who had entered my life, either briefly or for an extended period of time, I would naturally compare them to what it was I had always found in Bella. Staying true to form, I had done this when the subject of Joy had initially been broached. As usual, my ardor for Bella had remained intact, and just for having this day here once again I found myself humbled and thankful.

"That far away longing look," Bella said rising to her feet while she met my gaze.

"Longing it is," I began with deliberate and concentrated awareness of speech. "And on so many levels."

I smiled as Bella questioned again in what was more than a puzzled inquiry – it was more like a plea, "Must everything go unsaid?"

"Some we have said, some we imply, some must pass between our eyes without words."

"And why must this be?"

"Mostly for security and social convention," I managed to say.

"Security for whom?" she replied.

"For me mostly. Sometimes my own thoughts frighten me."

"Are they that terrible?"

"Not terrible at all, but by putting forth words to my feelings, I set myself up to be naturally defeated if the words are heard but not returned in some fashion."

"And you do not know by this time that the words would not be returned with the same conviction?"

"That is where the constraints of social convention enter into the picture. We are not in ancient days and faraway places. The reality of our existence is here and now. One of us is happily married, the other is not unhappy."

Bella smiled at me tenderly, "You know I love you."

"And I love you. You have always been dear to me and having this time right now in this cottage by the shore is so very beautiful." It seemed to me that by chance or design a love that spanned ages held us in that moment. We had been given a precious gift in each other, a fondness and closeness that happens too infrequently in today's society – and we both recognized how special this bond between us was, a bond that could only exist as it was in this age and this life.

Perhaps cruel destiny was not so cruel after all – the mutual love we shared with each other was not a blaze of desire that quickly burns out or relies upon passion to fuel the flame. The love shared here was different; it was a love that was not transitory in nature, but rather had grown over the course of a lifetime and would surely continue long after we have shed these mortal shells of flesh.

We parted slightly, each of us lost in our own thoughts and I instinctively wiped a tear from

Bella's cheek that had made its way down from her moist eyes. "We are something," I said with a smile on my face, trying to cover the pain of despair or missed desire.

Bella laughed and wiped her eyes on the sleeve of my shirt, "We are something all right..." she trailed off with a smile on her face. She turned and continued washing the few dishes we had used for breakfast, letting them air dry on a dish towel laid out upon the countertop the way it had always been done here.

"Will you stay late today, Bella?", I asked as I took a sponge to the Formica table and deposited a few crumbs of bread into the trash can under the sink.

"As long as I can. Alex has school tomorrow and Michael has work. I know they could get along without me another night, but they are so good to me, I want to send them off with a breakfast and good lunch packed. We still eat together every morning we can, and we get to eat dinner as a family, although Alex's wanderlust is just beginning to show itself. I swear he reminds me of you so much."

"How so?", I asked surprised.

"He can't sit still. Sometimes I think he'll be a great lawyer or ballplayer, and sometimes I think he'd be just as happy as a hobo jumping train to train across America picking fruit and working odd jobs. He gets that from all the stories you put into his head when you lived with us." Bella turned smartly around and pointed a finger at me in mock accusation. "You made him this way," a smile across her face.

"He's a great kid," I said as I refilled my coffee. "You've done such a wonderful job of raising him." I paused for a moment, "Michael, too. They really seem to have quite an affection for each other."

Bella: "Michael's been a Godsend. After you and Susan got married, I felt like I'd never be able to take care of Alex properly without a male role model. I always have been thankful for your support, and I know I'll never be able to repay you for your kindness to us."

"Nonsense. Bella, you are a part of me. I wish I could have done more for you."

"I'm sure Susan was hard to convince about that...let's go into the living room, it's so much brighter there."

Bella and I gathered up our coffee, and she grabbed a package of Royal Lunch Milk Crackers, the ones in the familiar purple box. These had always been a favorite of my grandparents and I wondered if we were the only people born after World War II that purchased this product.

We sat down in the living room next to each other on the large sofa. Bella pulled her legs up under herself and held the coffee mug with both hands. She was sitting sideways facing me, and despite the fact that she had not had much sleep nor had put on any makeup, she could rival any of Hollywood's most prominent beauties. She was wearing a pair of sweatpants and one of my sweatshirts, our size difference giving her a sprite-like appearance. I ate a couple of milk crackers, dipping them into my coffee, their crispiness immediately becoming soggy with the absorption of the liquid. I was apparently looking pensive as Bella asked me my thoughts.

"I was just thinking of the early years with Susan," I replied with an audible sigh. It's hard to believe that something so passionate could become so very mundane in such a short period of time."

"Go on," she said simply.

"Those days on the shore when you and I were taking care of Alex were the most wonderful days of my life. I don't know how it came to pass that Susan not only found me but was able to pull me away from here and away from you."

"She didn't pull you away from me," Bella quickly rejoined, partly to ease the pain she saw on my face and partly to fill in the gap of silence that had entered the room.

I continued, "I know, but I eventually did leave, and I left with her."

"You were in love."

"Was I?"

"You said you were."

"I was young." I ate another cracker, this time the soggy side falling into my coffee mug. "I hate it when you do that," I smiled, getting up to get a spoon. Bella laughed and sipped her coffee as I returned and took my seat next to her, fishing out the piece of cracker with the old monogrammed 'I' on it. I laughed.

"Mmmmm?", Bella said.

"Every time I see these assorted spoons and forks with the 'I' on them it just cracks me up," I said. Who else would get an 'I' for Italy on their flatware?

"Our grandfather was a riot," Bella laughed back, both of us remembering Noni saving S&H Green Stamps for a nice set of flatware she saw in the A&P advertisement. Noni had made the mistake of sending our grandfather to pick up the flatware while he was in Hartford at the S&H showroom when he took the twins to G. Fox's downtown.

When he returned, Noni couldn't believe there was no 'D' on her set of flatware, but an 'I'. Our grandfather explained that he took the 'I' flatware when the S&H clerk offered him a free toaster to take them off his hands. He said that 'I' stood for Italy anyway and couldn't quite understand his wife being so upset; after all, it was a new toaster. This flatware incident was laughed about for many years to come, Uncle Gino even labeling Noni's hairbrush and shoes with small letter "I's", getting a smack on the back of his head.

"It's chilly," Bella started, touching the windowpane with her delicate hand.

"Good day for a bonfire on the beach," I said.

"Those were so much fun. I don't think they let kids do that anymore except for the high school homecoming."

I leaned back on the sofa facing my cousin. "Kids are missing out," I ventured. "I guess everyone is a little more lawsuit happy than when we were younger."

Bella smiled coyly, "It was fun, but a bunch of kids playing with fire in the dark usually with beer or vodka probably wasn't the best of ideas anyway."

"You're just saying that because you fell off the roof!', I laughed.

Bella hit my arm, "You let go of me!" she said. "I still have gravel marks on my knees from the roof shingles."

4.

The incident we were referring to occurred when we were fourteen or fifteen years old, too young for the crowd that had gathered that weekend at the far side of the cove by the jetty and the pine trees. Every weekend it seemed that some group of kids would build a bonfire at the shore throughout that summer, and at least one or two during the school year. Nights like the one in question would find the under-twenties out in the crisp air, not too windy, the fire, alcohol, and body heat defenses against the coolness of the wind. The older kids would invariably show up with cheap beer – usually Pabst or Black Label – perhaps schnapps to be passed around. Couples would snuggle together, and someone always brought a ball for touch football. The weakest link would usually end up in the water or at the back end of some practical joke, but it was all good-natured fun, and despite the alcohol, most bonfires were never a problem; the local parents having participated in such pleasures at some time in their lives.

The incident Bella was referring to that had resulted in skinned knees and bruised egos was from our early teen years when we had been restricted from going to one of these bonfires. The restriction had been over some event involving my sister, Elizabeth and the twins. Bella and I had been sent upstairs to 'think things over a bit', much to the delight of the younger children. As we passed the time in a state of gloom, we were able to see the bonfire almost framed in the bedroom window.

It was calling to us, and as seafarers followed sirens to their eventual doom, Bella and I followed the silent call of the flame. We quickly opened the window, planning our escape from the wardens of our captivity. Being a quick decision, we did not take into account minute details such as the effect of the night's freeze on the damp shingled roof. With the window open and the breeze blowing, Bella and I began scrambling down the sloped roof of the cottage to our ultimate destination like two moths heading for a flame. And we were about to get burnt.

Bella had gone out first, taking each step slowly in deference to the aforementioned light freeze that had descended upon the cottage. I was holding Bella's right hand with my left, while I held onto the windowsill with my other hand, our eyes trying to adjust to the dark starless night. We were being as silent as possible, a few bumps and bruises, a necessary evil that would quickly fade to exhilaration when we reached the bonfire.

Or as I should say, had we reached the bonfire; for at that moment the door to our room swung open and Elizabeth and the twins noticed our whereabouts and began yelling, "Vincent and Isabella are on the roof! Mom! Dad! They're on the roof!" the younger children stood defiantly in front of the window, calling out to the adults below. My sister was just out of reach as I tried to grab onto her to either silence her screams or choke her, each option having merit at the time. Either way, I swung my body around to get a firm hold of the windowpane in an effort to quickly get inside. In a second I realized my mistake, as I had let go of Bella, and turned to see her slide down the roof, yelling my name. My eyes adjusted just quickly enough to see her dark outline tumble a few times and disappear over the edge of the roof, a distinct thud emanating from the unyielding and immovable ground below.

Uncle Sal and Aunt Mary had reached the landing and immediately comprehended the situation. As for her part, Elizabeth stayed eyes glued to the window over my shoulder to where Bella had just been. Both adults ran downstairs to where Bella's distinct cry could be heard. As for me, I hoisted myself inside, quickly formulating a story that would be plausible enough to explain Bella and myself being out on the roof at nine o'clock at night. It was then that I noticed Elizabeth being pushed aside and began to feel the distinct firm grip of my angry father's hand upon my shoulder, pulling me unceremoniously inside the cottage.

In one fluent move I was not only inside, but the twins and Elizabeth were swept out of the room as my pants were pulled knee level, the leather of my father's belt being vigorously applied with extreme precision to my rear end. Bella on the other hand, was being tended to by her parents and Aunt Mary and as I stood there taking quite a licking, I determined that I would have been better off had I fallen off the roof with her. I was also, between the sting of my father's belt, plotting revenge against my sister and the twins, the three of them standing just out of my father's view, making faces, and pointing at me.

Bella ended up being OK, just a few bumps and bruises that healed well and quickly, except for the gravel scars on her knees where she had slid down the roof before plunging over the side. And that was the misadventure of the bonfire as we later would remember it, both of us in some degree of discomfort and totally banned from anything that even sounded remotely like fun for the rest of the summer.

5.

I looked at Bella's smiling face. I realized that time was marching on, ever forward, and that despite my best efforts to repel its attacks, a sadness passed over my countenance. I imagined a time distant yet definite when Bella and I would naturally succumb to the fate of all that is mortal, and one of us would precede the other into the promised paradise. Although I have always believed that the beauty and wonders of eternity would somehow make this existence seem as but a beginning, I still had a moment of sadness when I realized that one of us would have to be waiting for the other at the pearly gates. This knowledge hurt, and my heart was saddened by the prospect, for although this world was only a reflection of what was to come, this world was a world I knew, was comfortable in, and contained the love I knew. Despite the turmoil and angst of this world, the thought of being separate from it burdened my heart.

Truth be known, I did not want to ever leave this cottage and this person, and if Heaven was imperfect that was OK, I'd take it like this, right here, right now, an eternity that would not miss a moment of what was so precious to me. I did not want to leave this place, and I did not want the cottage to slip through my fingers and away from my control. I did not want bulldozers to destroy the physical past associated with this place. I did not want my memories destroyed nor future dreams removed from my family. Most of all I wanted this now to be an eternal now, never having to close Bella's eyes when her spirit would travel to meet its Divine Maker, and her mortal shell would become once again the dust the original woman sprang from, only to inherit a "temporal' existence.

My heart hurt with this thought of final departure, and I breathed deeply with conviction, willing those bright blue eyes to always stay open, always be there for me. Against the warm and familiar backdrop of the cottage, I could not picture a moment when Bella and I would not tread the same road of existence at the same time. I was grieving for the hours I would spend apart from her, praying that I would precede her into the world to come, so my reality would always include her comforting being.

Bella noticed the look of anguish that had spread across my face, and lovingly asked, "Are you okay?".

I forced a smile to my lips, straightened up my posture and laughed slightly, "Yeah, I just don't want any of this to ever change."

Bella returned my smile, but hers was not forced but rather her smile reflected the total peace and acceptance of what life was to her. “They will change, Vincent. No matter what you decide about the cottage, life goes on. We only have so many moments allowed together that’s why they are so very precious. If we had unlimited time, we’d take things for granted.”

“I wouldn’t,” I protested sounding like an obstinate child.

“Eventually you would. Not just being at the cottage was always important to us – it was about returning to it, and the sense of anticipation of seeing our family together. I couldn’t wait to see you each summer and each winter break, and I’d count down the days until we’d leave for the shore. And the cottage would always be here for us. That was precious time – not just being here but anticipating what was waiting for me here.”

“I had to be away from the cottage to appreciate it?” I asked.

“Possibly to appreciate it with depth, anyway. If we weren’t forced away from each other, there would never be that wondrous joy we feel when we are in each other’s company. We have each other, but that’s special because sometimes we are apart.”

I sat and listened to my cousin, her words soothing my intellectual and spiritual quandary.

Yes. We would enjoy each other because we could always return, and that longing transcended age and it cheated death. This cottage was a constant in an ever-changing world, and the lives that interacted here became part of the allure, part of what seemingly called us back. Yes, people who visited this place would have dreams, fulfill vows, live, grow old, and eventually die. But part of them remained here, visible proof that their lives had occurred, had meant something, had been important to others. The cottage was a backdrop of many lives played across its stage and those lives in turn created the love and laughter that occurred here.

The cottage was the lifeblood of the family. It was meatballs and homemade gnocchi rolled with bare hands and a loving heart. This cottage was alive with my grandfather's passion for life itself, and held the zest from Noni's doing laundry on Friday so the clothes could air dry by Sunday Mass. It was Christmas dinners, birthday parties, and abstaining from chocolate during Lent. It was a wooden bench under an apple tree in a fenced backyard and a hand-dug cellar. It was Jimmy Carmichael showing up every Saturday at eight-thirty in the morning to bike into town and having to walk the bikes up the first hill because our legs were not strong enough to pedal up that hill, but we coasted smoothly down on the return trip to the cottage later in the day.

The cottage cultivated relationships from the first kiss of a summer's romance to a farewell kiss at a funeral. It was getting that special place next to that special cousin at Thanksgiving dinner; it was looking out for your little sister without her knowing it. The cottage was time spent with aunts and uncles that seemed eternal until one grew older and understood the temporary aspect of life.

Second cousins and best friends would crowd the small haven as Noni or one of the older Aunts made pizzelles on the antique pizzelle iron, the sweet smell of anise that would fill the cottage with its pleasant aroma for days. It was eggplants and tomatoes growing in a garden and lamb roasting in a gas oven. It was shouting and crying and laughing all at once; it was the cry of a newborn baby, and the mournful Rosary at death.

Boys departed from this place for wars and came back as men.

My grandfather had settled here, and Uncle Leo visited often. Bella and I always considered this home. Theresa went away one day and never came back. The cottage was constantly in motion but in the same fashion was immovable. Despite the comings and goings of so very many people, the cottage continued to accept more and more.

No matter what external influences congregated on the cottage's personage – for wasn't it alive? – the cottage would always respond with a welcome and incorporate both wisdom and folly into its wooden rafters.

Bella was looking at me serenely as I pulled myself out of this digression.

"Lots of memories here," she said.

I lifted my brows and smiled warmly. "How long was I out for?", I jested.

"Just a moment or two," she said. "Especially if you take into consideration all of the years you were thinking about."

I drank the last of my coffee. Bella was up quickly asking me if I wanted more.

"No, I'm good.," I said, still partially lost in my latest train of thought. "Do you think that they ever thought about how precious this place would become all those years ago?"

"I think it was precious to everyone; a place where the whole family could be together and feel loved," Bella said, returning from the kitchen. She sat down beside me and took my hand in hers. "It's almost eleven fifteen, do you want to get ready for mass?"

I smiled at Bella. "Yeah...I'll go upstairs and change real quick – you want me to wear a suit?"

"No, you'll be ok in slacks. I found your shirt yesterday and went ahead and ironed it."

I smiled at my cousin's attention to compassion and predictability. We had always gone to Mass on Sundays, at first a mandatory expression of Christian fidelity put upon us by our family that led to a sincere desire to attend services as we grew into adulthood. Father Malone was no longer a part of St. Mary's. He had been retired a few years ago, and from the occasional updates we received, he was enjoying life at a Catholic retirement home in Lakeland, Florida.

As I dressed, I thought about how alike my feelings were regarding the cottage and St. Mary's. Both were indelible parts of my personal history, both were subject to change, but neither really did. The people that frequented both places changed as the years ticked by, but the structure and function of each had remained constant. St. Mary's was a part of Branford; old, rustic, filled with the lives and loves of this town that had always gone to Mass there and whose descendants would always go to Mass there. The Church was not only a temple of the God it served, but it was also a temple of consistency. The pews were always oak, polished lovingly by the aged members, despite arthritis and despite the time it took. The altar was always a beautiful marble, and the stained glass was always breathtaking, from the small Madonna and Child to the full-size replica of the Church's patron Saint. Behind the altar was always the Resurrection of Christ, figuring prominently in the original design of the building. The beautiful colors that came through into the church bathed all in lights of oranges, greens, and purples that cast colorful shadows on the Stations of the Cross that adorned the interior walls and seemed to make the figures of stone living testaments to the holiness of this place.

There was a new priest, of course, a Father Al who liked to play the violin, and I thought for a moment on whether they retired Father Malone's robes like they retire the numbers of sports legends. Father Al spoke two languages, English and Spanish, so that the congregation could understand the sermons instead of the now antiquated Latin that Bella would grill me on for hours when we were at Catholic school, and I was an altar boy. Father Al would also face the congregation, addressing the faithful on a personal level, adding warmth to the congregation. The faces changed and adapted to the world around them, but the Church was the constant that brought them together, as was the cottage.

I was trying my shoes and readjusting my plain blue tie – no one ever wore jeans or T-shirts to St. Mary's and as I came down the stairs, Bella was waiting for me at the front door, her leather-bound copy of the St. Joseph's missal in her left hand. "Ready to go?" I asked, turning off the lights in the kitchen and checking the pilot light in the oven out of habit.

"All set," she said, as she grabbed the keys to her car. She was wearing a plain black dress that would have been considered sack-like on anyone else, but Bella's tiny frame and confident smile combined with the simple pearl necklace I had given her on her 40th birthday made her radiate beauty. "Thanks for going with me," she smiled, "it really means a lot to me."

I smiled back at her as we left the cottage, "Do you still go daily?" I asked.

"Most of the time. When the kids had to be at school at seven I kind of stopped until they could drive themselves, but I've been going at least twice a week now."

We locked the doors and went outside to Bella's car. I opened up the passenger side for her, and she gingerly slid in, her knees pulled tight together the way that only women familiar with wearing a dress know how to do. I closed the door behind her, unlocked the gate and then let myself into the car. We sat for a few minutes as the engine warmed up. I'm still not sure if this helps anything, but old habits die hard, and this was something my father had always insisted on. I put the car in reverse and backed out of the gravel driveway, heading toward the Church, about a ten-minute drive from the cottage.

I cracked the window about an inch to allow the fresh, crisp air to mingle with the artificial heat that was coming out of the car's dashboard vents. Bella smiled at me, her hand resting on top of the missal on her knees, just visible without obstruction, a cold first day of winter here in New England.

As we left the gravel road and drove onto Main Street, I could feel the coolness enter the window as it filled the car. Bella shuddered slightly and adjusted her sweater to cover most of her arm. I rolled the window up, and smiling at her, began the succession of right turns that took us into town, past the bread shop that was still closed on Sundays, past the giant supermarket and into the parking lot of St. Mary's, where congregates of the early Mass were leaving to go about their daily business of whatever lives they were leading; watching a ballgame, cooking a special dinner or possibly taking a day trip to Hartford or Boston.

I parked Bella's car, turned off the engine and walked around to the passenger's side where my cousin sat patiently waiting for me. I relished the feeling of once again being the one who was taking care of her, opening her door, taking her hand for support, walking arm in arm. She was a lady in every sense of the word, and while she was not above a little mischief every now and then, she never crossed that invisible line that would allow anyone to speak unflattering of her or ascribe to her anything but the most favorable reports.

But Bella was devout, and took her time here as sacred, and as we walked into the Church her eyes were heavenward, making the sign of the cross with the Holy Water. I smiled to myself as I genuflected by our pew, wondering what it would be like to always have eyes fixed on you, always under scrutiny, and I marveled at Bella's composure. I took the aisle seat next to her as she slid in to give me room. And, as we had done since childhood, pulled down the padded kneeler and began our silent prayers to her Creator and mine, asking first for penance, then reflecting on what were our special needs.

I sat wondering what Bella's prayers would be like. I finished my prayers and sat back in the pew watching Bella's eyes shut. She looked so peaceful, and I realized had she not met Lucas so very long ago, my cousin would probably have taken vows. Sensing my stare, Bella smiled, sat back, and said as if I had asked the question out loud that she was busy giving thanks for what she had in her life.

We opened the missal to the reading of the day and stood as the bell chimed the entrance of Father Al and the congregation joined the chorus in the opening song, one that most of us cradle to grave Catholics had memorized many years ago.

The amiable priest entered the walkway behind a Crucifix carried by and altar girl, again a change from our childhood. Father Al was a refreshingly personable priest; I've known quite a few that were sociable at gatherings, but solemn to the point of coolness during Mass. Perhaps the solemnity of the surrounding icons and organ music tends to temper their temperament, perhaps their surroundings creating an environment of solemnity that is not to be found in other denominations. It's reverent, and I try to take Susan and our son at least once a month to a local service.

The quietness of the Catholic Mass is what appealed to me, no one ever yelling at us from the pulpit (except when teenagers would come in dressed inappropriately), no one visiting our home unannounced, no one trying to be my best friend. The closest I got to anyone was the "Peace be with You" greeting just after the Sunday collection. I could have joined the Knights of Columbus, and Susan actually did work a soup kitchen a few times, but the tone here was of somber respect. Respect and prayer wrapped up in a fifty-five-minute engagement.

The Mass was predictable and purposeful. Father Al alluding briefly to the weather and the start of the Christmas Season, and prayers were offered up in accordance with rite and tradition. I found it comforting to be here in this familiar place, and as the Mass ended, Father Al left the sanctuary to meet his congregation in the foyer as they said their last prayers and filed out of the oversized wooden doors.

As I stood, Bella took my arm in hers and gently led me to the quiet prayer room, where she lit two candles for the intentions of her caring heart. The statue of the Sacred Heart and Bella's calmness, I sat watching from a back pew, were both serene and otherworldly. The room was fragrant with the burning candles, and I smiled comparing it to the Cathedral in Florida where on and of switches turned a faux candle into what was here a fragrant offering. Staring at the real flame and smelling the scents were miles away from looking at a little bulb inside a red glass cover that could only be removed by the appropriate key. Not everything had changed for the better I decided.

Bella blessed herself, rose and approached me. "Thank you for being here," she said, again wrapping her arm around mine.

"Of course. You know I enjoy going to Mass with you."

"Do you normally go with Susan?"

"Susan doesn't quite 'get' being a Catholic" I smiled.

Bella patted my arm. "We can always hope she'll turn around. I know it would be important to you. I take Alex every week and Michael usually joins us."

We walked back to Bella's car, Bella pulling her sweater tightly around her small frame against the cool breeze. I adjusted my coat too, the crispness of the air chilling my body, and causing us to unconsciously walk faster. We passed several people hurrying in for the 1 p.m. Spanish Mass acknowledging each other with a nod of the head or a quick hello. The glances at Bella continued, people noticing the distinct glow about her personage. In a different life she would have made her vows; but perhaps it was better this way, able to help others along their paths without being taken out of society for a life of prayer and reflection.

I opened the car door for her. "Where to?"

"Let's grab some lunch together somewhere," she said as she slid into the passenger seat.

"Friendly's or something fancy?", I asked recalling her ill-fated summer job as a hostess at one of the New England restaurants' locations.

"Actually, I could go for a good slice of pizza," she smiled as I started the engine and turned the heater on.

"A woman after my own heart."

I began to pull out of the Church's parking lot, the sky having changed to a damp-looking grey as is normal here in the Northeast. There was moisture in the air, and had it been ten degrees cooler, the light mist that was collecting on the windshield would probably have been snowflakes. Bella opened up her black "Church purse" and put on a pair of dainty black gloves, adjusted her makeup in the mirror behind the sun visor, and satisfied with herself, leaned back in the leather seat.

Apizza was doing a brisk business, its small oval tables filled with happy patrons glad for the good food as well as the warmth being emitted from the pizza oven. Red and white checkered tablecloths adorned each table and booth, old wine bottles filled with artificial flowers keeping watch over the grated cheese and hot pepper. We took a small booth for two in front of the window, and each grabbed a menu.

"I am so looking forward to this," I said with obvious anticipation on my face.

"Didn't you have this delivered to you yesterday?" Bella asked as she removed her gloves and then her sweater.

"Yeah, but today's a new day," I said, taking off my coat and looking at the selection of grinders that Apizza was serving today, visions of the foot long sandwiches dancing in my head.

A young girl of perhaps seventeen or eighteen with jet black hair and red rose lipstick approached our table. Despite the cold weather she was wearing the Apizzashort-sleeved shirt with her faded blue jeans and an old apron tied around her waist, a few straws in the front left pocket. The waitresses at Apizza had always looked like this, young and pretty, dark complexions and usually chewing gum. They always knew the small menu by heart, as did most of the clientele, and after the first week or so they never carried anything to write the orders on. Orders were still yelled back to the cooks, and I had always marveled at the fact that not only had I never had a bad meal here at Apizza, I had also never had any mistakes with my food.

6.

Her name badge said Amelia, and she was a local girl on break from school. She had worked here for three winters already, starting when she was in high school. Bella smiled accommodatingly as I found out a little about our server Amelia; small talk that was almost expected when going out for dinner in a locally run restaurant, similar to the idle chatter that takes place when paying for gas – neither party really concerned about what they are saying. I ordered each of us a birch beer soda, knowing how much my cousin enjoyed this simple break from a strict water and juice diet. Because of the chill outside that had settled in my bones, I ordered a cup of minestrone soup. Bella mouthed the words 'no thank you' as she shook her head. I asked Amelia if we could have the soup and drinks first and then order lunch. Assuming Bella was my wife, the young waitress complimented Bella on her diamond ring and band, letting us know that she was getting married during summer recess. Bella smiled, and I thanked her for the compliment and told her that I hope she was as happy as we were. I made a mental note to tip her a little more than I normally would have.

The cold birch beer and hot minestrone arrived, Amelia placing a small loaf of fresh bread and olive oil between the two of us. "Ready to order?", the young girl asked, fixing her eyes on Bella.

"I'll have a small antipasto and a side of angel hair in a meat sauce," she answered. I smiled. Bella had been ordering the same thing at this restaurant for the past twenty years. If you find something you like, stick with it, I thought.

Amelia turned to me. "I'll have the sausage and pepper grinder," I said.

"Half or whole?"

"Look at the size of me," I smiled, my six foot, two-hundred-pound frame calling out for the large sandwich.

Amelia laughed obligatorily, and went to the next table, our orders somehow stored in a compartment in her brain dedicated to Apizza orders. Bella smiled, "You're still a flirt," she laughed.

I tried my best to look shocked. "I'm aghast," I said, "and she's young enough to be my daughter...and I am a happily married man."

"One who is forever unsatisfied with his life and constantly tries to change the outcome of whatever you set your mind trying desperately to reach a place that may or may not even exist."

Bella pulled a piece of bread and dipped it in the oil and oregano mixture. I took a sip of birch beer as I contemplated her insight. Deciding that what she had espoused was perhaps true, I said, "Am I really that unsatisfied?"

"You make yourself that way. You just can't see over the hill, so you go running up at full speed only to find another hill. Plus, you like to flirt," she smiled. "It's always funny to watch you turn on your charm whenever you think someone is cute, which is okay because you actually dote on me more than anyone else."

"That's because I love you best," I said.

"I know. That's why Michael and you don't get along so well, and Susan and I never became close friends."

I ate a little of the warm soup and buttered a pulled piece of bread. "Susan likes you," I said to the bread with no real conviction.

Bella smiled. "She likes me because you want her to like me. She knows that I am important to you."

"And Michael?" I asked, already knowing the answer.

"Michael is a good man and a wonderful husband and father. He just really doesn't care for you," a sly smile creeping across her face, "Good soup?".

I laughed out loud as I saw the sparkle in Bella's eye again. "I'm glad to finally hear it. All these years of wondering and I finally know that my efforts to be his pal have all been for naught."

Bella laughed too, pointing an accusing finger at me, "You knew from the first time we all went out that he'd never be your best friend. You and I danced that night more than Michael and I did."

"Well, I didn't know you were going to marry him," I said with conviction.

"Mmm...I guess that is so. But Doctor Psychiatrist Cousin of mine, do you really think a man's ego can ever get over being second place?"

"Well, professionally...." I began....

"Yes?"

"Professionally I think I'll finish this soup."

"Did I mention that you are a master of avoiding being questioned yourself?"

"Only when I get all squirmy inside," I answered.

"Eight years of college and ten years of private practice, and the best you can come up with is squirmy?"

I laughed again. And there it was, right in front of me, what it always came back to and started from. Two people who loved being together and anticipated the other's needs. Whether it was breakfast with her son just before the Red Sox game or Bella making sure the pleats of my pants were perfectly creased before sending me out to see a client – we truly cared for each other. It was more than anyone could ever hope for – finding completion in another, as cold must be experienced to understand what warmth is.

I finished my soup with Bella's help and sipped on my soda. Amelia promptly returned to take away the empty bowl and informed us that our food would be out momentarily. The kitchen was a little backed up with the after-church crowd.

Bella waited until our waitress had walked away to give the same message to the other tables and I began, "When was the last time you remember seeing Uncle Leo?"

"Kind of out of the blue..." I said.

"Yeah, but every time I keep thinking about why we're here today, I can't help but think of all the memories of the shore and the people who are part of those memories. I just can't remember Uncle Leo that well. I see his granddaughter Angela every so often at the market, and we've had her up to the house once or twice. They live near Yale too."

"I haven't seen him since probably the last reunion, and that was at least five years ago. He looked ancient then...I guess I thought he must have died, although I suppose someone would have said something to me," I said.

"Angela mentions him sometimes, I think he lives with Angela's mother, Aunt Janet, in Coventry up by the University."

Uncle Leo was Noni's brother – an older brother who had to be in his mid-nineties. I found it refreshing to hear Bella say so matter-of-factly that he was still going strong, living with his youngest daughter who was herself at least seventy-five or six. In my profession many patients seek counseling to work through the guilt – or lack of guilt – that can accompany putting a loved one in a nursing home or managed care center. The thought of that happening in our family was never even a possibility. Grandparents, aunts and uncles, fathers and mothers, cousins, and siblings – all were equal parts of this living family right up to that final breath, that ending heartbeat.

More often than not, most family members of advanced years would move in with one of their children. If day to day care was needed, the son or daughter would take care of them. This, I felt, was also a blessing, as the aging relative could not only spend time with sons and daughters, but the mutually beneficial raising of children created an indelible link through generations. The elders could babysit the children, entertain them with stories about their own youth when milk was a nickel and was left on your porch door by the Hood Dairy Milkman. It was a very symbiotic relationship and allowed beautiful exchanges of stories and ideas that I felt most cultures miss out on by depositing their loved ones in a sanitized hospital to be taken care of by complete strangers who may or may not really give a rat's backside about the wellbeing of the loved one in question. Sure, there were instances when a family could not take proper care – senility and Alzheimer's causing the relative to become a danger to themselves or others, but just because someone turned seventy, it did not mean they were ready to be put out to pasture.

"The reunion was fun," I said. "I remember having that every year until the family kind of spread out away from New England."

Bella nodded, "Then they became less frequent and would be the only way to get us all together at the cottage or the Italian American Club. I liked it better when we just got together every weekend or so and everyone would invade the cottage."

"Summers too," I added.

"That's what I mean," my cousin continued as Amelia brought out our hot grinders and macaroni. She also filled our drinks and, rightly judging the importance of our conversation, simply asked us if we needed anything else. I told her no thanks and continued listening to Bella. "We used to get the whole summer or Christmas break, then everyone began to move away, and we started having reunions on Noni's birthday. When she died, we'd get together with those who lived nearby or every five years or so meet at a location between the North and the South. A couple of days at a hotel never really could compare to what we grew up with."

I ate a bite of the sausage and pepper sandwich. It seemed that Apizza still used the same recipes that were apparently handed down from God himself. It was delicious. Piping hot on a homemade toasted bun with red sauce and plenty of cheese. I burned my palate as I began to inhale this manna. I took a quick drink of birch beer and let an ice cube stay in my mouth.

"Careful, looks hot," Bella said, smiling as she daintily began her lunch.

After putting out the fire in my mouth, I began where we had left off. "You're right. I love the reunions. It's great to get everyone, or at least almost everyone, together and dance and sing and eat and drink Sangria while we tell stories about forty years ago, and we can watch our children make the memories that they will be talking about when it's their turn to be us." I drank some of my soda, "Although I do feel that the real reunion comes after the party when we all kind of gravitate back to the cottage for cards and biscotti. The past seems to stay at the door and new memories are being made; it's like life is beginning anew. These are the times I long for with our children when everyone knows that what we have together as a family is special. Sometimes Theresa even shows up."

Bella was nibbling some capicola from her antipasto, finishing the black olives first and working up to the macaroni. Now, after my lengthy discourse, she began to look at the Genoa salami. Her soft blue eyes were pensive. "That's why being here today is so precious for me, and I don't envy your decision tomorrow."

I stopped eating momentarily and thought about what she had just said. I'd been doing a lot of that lately. "Bella," I began, "it's not my decision – I just happen to be the one representing the majority of the family's wishes."

Bella smiled and took a small bite of a piece of ham.

"What?" I asked.

"Whose wishes?" she asked gently.

"The majority of the family," I said again, this time hoping to sound more convincing.

"The majority of the family that doesn't come to the cottage, or the majority of the family who this cottage really is important to, whether alive like you and me, or part of its history like Uncle Gino and Noni? We all deserve our respect and dignity whether we are memories or becoming memories."

Bella picked up another black olive and slowly ate around the pit. Our waitress approached, looked at the intensity of the expressions on our faces and bypassed our table.

Bella had a point. Sure, there were more relative desiring the sale of the cottage on this side of the ground, but shouldn't I also be a spokesman for those who went before us, an advocate for those who were now only pictures in albums, and fond memories? I was somehow representing a view that I did not share as I considered the interests of those who never took anything away from the cottage because they never put themselves into the cottage.

But it was different for Bella and me. The cottage was special because it was the place where we came into ourselves. It was Theresa's because it was the one place left on earth that she could recapture the lost innocence of youth. It belonged just as much to Elizabeth and Gina because this place was where Tina died, and their young lives were forever changed in an instant that showed them mortality was a human condition. And, as Bella said, the cottage belonged to people that were now with us as memories and pictures instead of being there physically. The cottage was Nono's, and Uncle Leo's. It was Uncle Gino's and despite his shortcomings, it was my father's. And maybe this was the realization he had hoped I'd figure out for myself after his death. Saddling me with the responsibility of the cottage maybe just wasn't one last thing to stick me with from beyond the grave, maybe, just maybe, it was a chance for me to understand that despite all the ups and downs of life, there was always love here. And perhaps I was the one most able to show that the cottage still stood for the love, comfort, and stability it had always represented. Maybe this was the final act of my father in a moment of clear understanding. He wasn't being malicious -he was entrusting to me a great responsibility. The burden I now had on my shoulders had been carried on the shoulders of men and women that I had always admired and respected, enjoyed being with, and loved. Maybe, just maybe, it was my turn to step in and fill a much-needed void, to be an impetus for positive change, instead of letting this vault of precious memory be unceremoniously destroyed forever.

Bella was smiling at me, "Penny for your thoughts."

"You apparently are aware of my thoughts dear cousin, and if I did not know you better, I'd say your entire trip here this weekend was in the hopes of encouraging such thoughts."

"Thoughts such as realizing the importance of keeping what belonged to the family in the loving hands of those to whom such memories actually mean something?" Bella quizzed in a teasing fashion, batting her doe-like eyes.

"Does Michael ever outmaneuver you?" I asked.

"Not a chance," came the reply, as Bella rolled the last of her pasta on the large spoon that always accompanies macaroni dishes in Italian restaurants.

I laughed a bit, ate the last of my delicious sandwich and motioned for Amelia to present us with our bill. Bella was patting the corners of her mouth with a paper napkin. As I looked at the bill, she produced a compact mirror and some red lipstick from her small purse, then gingerly applied it. She gave her eyes and makeup a quick once over in the small mirror, then, apparently passing her own evaluation, closed the mirror and returned it to her purse. I paid the bill with my MasterCard, making sure I left Amelia enough of a tip to cover our extended stay at her table, and helped Bella out of her chair. Apparently, the tip was satisfactory, for the young waitress came back to thank us for being so generous. Bella smiled at her, and we left Apizza together.

7.

I've always thought it amusing how the most mundane experiences can serve as focal points in life. Bella's closing of her mirror compact with its distinct 'snap' was really the final triumph of Bella over me regarding the cottage. In her mind it was over, what she had needed to say, she had said, and however I used her advice was no longer an issue for her, it was no longer in her control. Everything regarding the cottage was now up to me and she could now go home to her husband and son. Sure, she could stay another day, but with the cottage – that conversation had already occurred, and she had closed the discussion when she closed the compact.

Seemingly innocuous gestures could be this profound if people stopped to think about all the little things that added the flavor of opinion to most decisions. Noni's dying had indeed been monumental and had stayed with me as any major family death would naturally be expected to do, but it wasn't final in my mind's eye until I signed the Family & Visitors of the Deceased book in the front of All Saint's Funeral Chapel. It was one signature amongst many others, but with a simple stroke of a ballpoint pen, I realized that she was gone. Happier events were dotted with these small indelible memories also, the minute details of a major event establishing some major change in my life, a paradigm shift to a more mature vision of self. I remembered my first kiss, not so much for the kiss itself, but I clearly remember Uncle Gino taking me down to Bradlee's where I spent my life savings of fifteen dollars to buy Laura Cusco a stainless-steel bracelet. I remember the white box and pretty silver bow that the clerk had tied for us. Uncle Gino made me feel like a grownup, recognizing this monumental moment in my young life, something I've tried to do with my son. Uncle Gino refrained from teasing me and made me feel special, although I'm sure the clerk and my uncle traded some knowing smiles and glances at each other.

We went right from Bradlee's to the Cusco house where Laura lived with her grandparents. It was a Saturday afternoon and snowing lightly. Uncle Gino let me out a couple of houses away from Laura's, and I all but ran to her door, slipping and sliding on the ice that had formed when the sun had melted the afternoon snow and the cool day froze the water. I collected my thoughts, looked back at the idling car with exhaust coming out of the tailpipe. I exhaled deeply and rang the frozen doorbell. I then took a step back and fell down on my rear. Feeling embarrassed but not half as embarrassed as when I tried to get up, recovered my balance and realized Mr. Cusco was standing at the open door, asking me what I was doing in the snow on his front lawn without any gloves or a hat on. Mercifully, Laura smiled from behind her grandfather, taking a step out to the porch and said hello to me. I was up in a moment, handed her the white box with the pretty silver bow, muttered something that I hoped came out as Merry Christmas, leaned forward and gave her a quick kiss on her lips. Then I ran. Falling a couple of times, trying to get to Uncle Gino's car, an adrenaline rush consuming my body. I had kissed Laura Cusco! My now favorite uncle smiled at me and let me blab on like a fool for as long as it took for me to know that what I had done had somehow changed me.

Apparently, the little things were not so little after all. How many memories of the cottage and those that lived there flooded back to me whenever I saw contact paper lining an elderly person's flatware drawer? What part of me relived the memories tucked neatly away when I saw a Coke in a glass bottle, instead of plastic? The smell of anise that reminded me immediately of making pizzelles with Aunt Josie? We'd share a bottled Coke and used wooden kitchen utensils that came from a contact paper lined drawer.

It was all related somehow. Major special times were always remembered like birthdays and

Christenings, weddings, and funerals. But there was a deeper level that I had now understood as I opened Bella's car door. At that moment, I realized that the little events could be the most precious, the memories of everyday life that somehow came together to form what it was like to be alive.

It was Jujubees at the cinema and later at the multiplex. It was a snowball that caught you unexpectedly. It was the steam from a radiator and learning how to change your own oil on your first car, and a Creamsicle bought off a Good Humor truck. Stray cats showing up at the doorstep, the way the rain dripped down from the gutter and filtered down into a small clay pot Noni had put under its lip. It was leaving screen doors open and swimming at the shore getting stung by jellyfish.

For the first time in my adult life, I was able to wrap my mind around what life really was to me. Life was a constant stream of unrelated small events that never took more than it gave. All parties involved in an event were affected if some manner or fashion, adding to the richness and flavor of their lives. I remembered reading a book by Richard Grant that said that life was this and that and everything else mixed together all at once. I finally understood what he had meant. Everything that I was at this moment came from the little and often unremembered events of my daily life, and my relationships with others. Not only that, but this knowledge looked forward as well as backwards; every action that I would ever take from this moment on would somehow form the life I would lead tomorrow and the next day, and upon my death, the intricacies would somehow affect the lives of many others who in their lives were living all the minute happenings that were defining them as unique individuals. And so on forever.

I started the car after making sure that Bella was wearing her seat belt and arrived shortly at the cottage with a full stomach and an equally full brain. Despite the climax of the sun's journey across the sky, the temperature had dropped about ten degrees since we left for Mass this morning. I unlocked the front door and Bella and I quickly entered the warm living room.

"Thank you," I said simply as I hung up my coat in the hall closet, the stale air quickly mingling with the freshness of the room.

Bella was taking off her sweater, her small shoulders turning a lovely pinkish color from the change in temperature. I watched her fold the sweater neatly and place it on the corner of the couch, put her black purse on top of it, then stretch fully, her hands reaching up to heaven as she stood on her tiptoes and arched her back.

"You're welcome," Bella said as she continued to stretch. "That lunch was delicious. We've been going there thirty years and I've yet to be disappointed." She slipped off her shoes and dug her toes into the carpet, her black hose bunching at her feet. "I'm tired."

"You look tired," I said.

"Thanks," she smiled, "I was up all night with your inner child."

"Ouch," I said, "but I guess you were. Are you going to nap?"

"Yeah...I'll lay down for an hour or so. That way I'll be rested up for the drive home later."

"You could stay an extra night," I said.

"Hmmm...I'd love the company, but Michael and Alex need me."

"They're very lucky."

"So you say...", smiling, Bella reached out and grabbed my hands. "Pull my back a moment, won't you?"

"Sure," I said, taking her small hands in mine and leading her to the sofa. She laid face down with arms extended as I slowly pulled her arms toward me.

"I won't break," she said, her arms now hyper-extended.

I laughed. "You're just so small; I'm always scared to pull too hard." I continued for a few minutes, then let her arms relax.

Bella turned to face me as I now sat next to her on the floor. “Thanks, you always make me feel wonderful, and I love you for it.”

I smiled at my cousin. Bella closed her eyes and was asleep in ten minutes. I sat and watched her sleep. Totally relaxed, her stretching had eliminated anything that may have bothered her, but few things ever did. She was a wonderful *person*.

Rising to my feet with a small groan of impending age, I went upstairs and changed from church clothes to something less formal, and old sweatshirt with UCONN fading across the front, matching sweatpants, and my running shoes. Back downstairs, I looked over at my sleeping cousin, smiled and went out into the bright cold afternoon.

Although a flood of thoughts swirled in my mind, I felt strangely better; I felt as though a burden had been lifted off my shoulders. I somehow knew that whatever I did regarding the cottage was not only for others, but for myself, too. And that was ok. Any action I took, or did not take, wasn’t the vague and cloudy fulfillment for people I had not seen in years. My decision here affected me in a very personal and real way. While I was acting as agent of the collective will of the family, I was acting for myself as well, and I was the only one who would actually have to live with my actions. I felt as though I was being asked to put down a favorite dog who had become old and distant, not for the dog's sake, but because it would make my life easier.

This place was a part of me, this place housed the memories that sustained me through difficult times in a real and tangible way. Bulldozers could never destroy the memories that were associated with the cottage – but they could destroy the physical place itself, and that all-important feeling one receives from tactile contact that held memories in a never-ending embrace. Like a person, the body could be destroyed and sever the earthly bonds that had been a life while slowly causing memories to blur and fade over time. I did not know whether I was truly ready to let go of the 'life' of the cottage and cause its memories to be set adrift.

I had instinctively crossed the road and was heading down to the jetty when a shout from the street startled me back into the present moment. I was surprised I had come this far. Because of the position of the sun, I could barely make out the person's figure, but as I put my hand to shade my eyes, I could tell it was Jimmy Carmichael, approaching with one of his dogs on a leash.

"Hey Vincent," he called waving one hand as the black lab pulled on the other.

"Say Jimmy," I returned, making a waving gesture.

The greeting ritual passed, Jimmy and his dog continued on their way, perhaps in some way sensing that it was solitude I was searching for, and not a conversation. I was happily relieved at his apparent insight, and I continued on to the jetty, quite easily navigated in the bright afternoon sun. I shook my hands to warm them and advanced to the rocks end at the cool ocean. It was high tide, and the water was a beautiful greenish blue. Small waves unceasingly lapped the rocks as I settled down in the same place I had sat last night, but with a much different inner feeling. The sun was to my back, and the seemingly endless sea stretched out before my eyes. The water was a perfect metaphor for life here in Branford: it continued indefinitely, and despite its appearance, was constantly changing right below the surface. In some places it was warm and colorful, in other places it was dark and forbidding. It was filled with life, but also contained death. It was pleasurable and filled with purpose, giving life and in return receiving life back into itself.

It was forever.

The coolness of the day did not bother me, and I was in a better and clearer frame of mind after my conversations with Bella. Last night it was dark, today the ocean seemed especially fluid and clear. The sounds of the gulls were bits of laughter in the air, the sun's rays crystallized the top of each wave, each a precious gem that contained a mini universe of life and resurrection. The sound of the small waves where I sat was a symphony in practice to my ears and the taste of salt in the air was sweeter than the finest confectionary treat in Paris. As I sat there this Sunday afternoon, Bella fast asleep in the warm cottage. I felt a sense of completion that I had not felt in years. It was as if I had been asleep and awoke to find myself in a wonderful place that I thought I could only dream about. I thanked God that this was my reality.

And that was the beauty and truth of this special place in this special existence. I loved it here, and I needed this place to exist, not just in thought, but in actuality. Forget about the widening of the road or the new supermarket or the closing of the bait store. They had all chosen their future and created their own destiny. Now it was my turn, and despite obligation and responsibility to the family I was acting agent for, I found that I had a larger obligation and responsibility to those that went before me, to Bella, and in the end...to myself.

The wind blew cold and steady against my face. Billowing white sails dotted the crystal sea as pleasure-seeking boaters went about enjoying the afternoon. It was truly a gorgeous day, and the relief I felt in my heart added to the wonder and joy of my physical surroundings. Sitting alone on the jetty I felt an unusual sense of belonging, one that I had not felt for many years. I was not alone. Loving arms and gentle hands from across space and time gently held and caressed my being. I absentmindedly tossed a few stones into the water, watched a couple of pine needles fall to the ground, and gazed at a flock of seagulls searching for a meal. For the first time in many years, I just sat. I wasn't anxious or restless, my mind didn't drift into the plight of man's earthly condition, and I did not get stuck in the quagmire of moralities I was forced to think about during my working life. For this moment, for this now, I just *was*. In its simplicity it was remarkable, and its solitude was restful. I let my mind drift out over this glass-like sea, far away, but kept it anchored firmly in this here and now.

I thought of Theresa and the relevance of her call, and dreamed it was to bring her back to this safe place she held in her mind. I thought about my sister Elizabeth, and despite our age difference, we now had a very dear relationship as adults, a relationship that was drawn tighter as the years passed. Perhaps she would be able to take a vacation here with Susan and all our collective children, allowing them to establish the bonding of family like we were fortunate enough to have growing up.

The shadow and specter of my father was lifted – I could be myself and like who I was. Causing me to be here and live with my decisions seemed almost as if the man decided to open my eyes after his death and look at how life really was.

I thought of the possibility of frequent reunions for the cousins and second cousins that were separated by many miles. I imagined friendships and relationships flourishing here again at the shore. And wouldn't the older generation love to come back and visit and tell stories? Wouldn't Aunt Felice and Uncle Sal like to once more be included at a Christmas dinner with the laughter of the young children and the admiration of the adults? Wasn't this all worth working towards? Didn't the benefits of family togetherness outweigh a few dollars that would pass without notice? What price could truly be placed on this cottage that would be worth losing what we had always taken for granted? Did those favoring selling the cottage really consider what this piece of property really contained…the wealth of the years lived and loved?

Jimmy Carmichael passed by heading in the opposite direction from which he and his dog were going when they first passed me. Apparently on his way back home, I could tell from my peripheral vision that he had stopped and looked at me, but I kept staring out at the water, and did not turn around. The wind blew through my hair and my fingers were becoming cold, but still I just sat there, motionless, and for the first time in many years I was at ease with myself.

I noticed the holes in the coral rocks with small crabs and sea snails, I noticed brown seaweed collecting at the base of the jetty, with the small school of silver fish looking for food. I noticed the foam created only for a moment as a small wave inched over the reef. I noticed that smoke was coming out of the chimney of the house on the small island in the cove. I sat thinking and not thinking, for what could have been years, but in actuality was only a little more than an hour and a half.

8.

Pine needles lightly crunched behind me, and a slight shadow covered the sun. A small hand reached out and placed itself gently on my shoulder. The fingers squeezed with a knowing warmth.

"Hey," Bella said.

I smiled. "Hey," I said, turning to the only other person in the world that I would be able to share this moment with.

"Can I sit?"

"The ground's a bit on the chilly side."

"That's okay." Bella sat down next to me, wearing a heavy red checkered flannel coat, sweatpants and gloves. "Aren't you cold?", she asked, cuddling up next to me for warmth.

"I honestly hadn't thought about it," I answered. "Did you sleep well?"

"Yeah. I guess I was tired, I fell asleep so quickly. I felt as if I was where I belonged."

"I'm glad the cottage is comforting to you," I said as I looked into her eyes.

"It is," she said as I put my arm around her, and we were both silent for a few minutes.

"I'm glad you came," I said, staring off into a distance that I could not see.

"Me too. You know I have to leave soon. I want to make it home before dark, and and these winter days are always so short."

"Too short. I could spend another week here and it still would not be enough."

Bella held my hand, "You can make that happen."

"Not easily," I replied.

"True. But I've seen you do some pretty amazing things once you put your mind to them." She squeezed my hand and stood up. "Come and walk me to my car."

I obediently rose to my feet, a few of my bones creaking from stiffness, and my left foot was asleep. As I stood there letting the blood circulate by shaking my foot I said, "Tough to get old." Bella was of course light on her feet, almost elfishly spry.

"You are aging quite gracefully," she said, a warm smile following. "No gray hairs and only a few pops when you stretch. You've got a few good years left in you."

"I hope so!" I exclaimed as I laughed aloud. "I'm still the biggest and strongest, you know." I grabbed Bella and easily picked her up in my arms and carried her off the jetty.

"You'll see who the strongest is if you drop me," she laughed.

"Water looks mighty cold," I said, a slight grin creeping across my face.

"You wouldn't dare!", she said as she started to squirm in my arms.

"No, I would not," I said, "but it's still good to know that you think I still might."

"Just based on past experience!" She lightly hopped out of my arms and hugged me. "I've really got to hit the road."

"I know," I said as I took her hand in mine and we began walking back to the cottage.

Almost childlike in her demeanor as she skipped along by my side. Bella said, "I'm glad I was able to be here for you."

"It really made a difference, you know."

"We'll see," she said.

Bella and I waited at the road for a couple of cars to pass, crossed the street, and walking up the driveway, reached her car. "Know that you are loved," she said to me.

"I do", I said, noticing that her overnight bag was already in the backseat of the Volvo. "No way I can convince you to stay?"

"My work here is done," she laughed and threw her arms around my neck in a comforting embrace that was unique to our relationship.

I opened the car door for her, and she gracefully slid into the front seat, turned the key in the ignition, and adjusted the heat vents that I had earlier closed. Even in her mid-forties, she could pass for thirty, and her childlike movements added to her charm and the illusion of perpetual youth. She buckled herself in and adjusted the mirror as I squatted down beside her...the engine's low hum somehow comforting.

"Give me a call later and let me know you made it home safely," I said.

"I always do," she smiled, leaned over, and kissed my cheek.

"Thanks Bella, my best to Michael and Alex."

She pouted playfully, "I thought I had your best..." she said.

"You always will," I replied, standing up.

"I know." She closed the door, put the car in reverse, and edged out of the gravel drive. I stood watching her pull the car into the street heading further north toward I-95, as she beeped twice and waved.

It was about four o'clock and although I was alone again, Bella's memory stayed with me, and I knew it would always remain special and lasting, regardless of what happened tomorrow with the broker. I would remain loved. And I knew that was something so special and so unusual in this modern society of half-truths and a very low concept of what 'loved' actually meant.

It was a wonderful feeling to be needed in this life, and as I put my hands in my pockets, I mentally made notes of this feeling that I knew would never fade. Perhaps I could somehow apply this to some of my patients who were hanging on for themselves; maybe they needed to let the right person into their lives.

I walked inside the cottage, took off my sweatshirt and warmed myself for a few moments standing by the radiator. As I stood facing the wall, I noticed in the mirror's reflection that a card had been placed on the kitchen table, along with a vase of beautiful flowers.

I smiled as I walked over to the table and opened the card.

"My dear Vincent," it began, *"I wanted to tell you what it is that I think you already know. You must always follow your heart. That is what brought me to you on this occasion, and I want you always to continue your compassion towards others, while remaining true to the desires of your own heart. Keep the love that has brought you this far, and whatever choice you decide to make regarding the cottage, your family and I will always love you, and will always remain true to you."* It was signed, *"All my love, 'Bella'"*.

Despite its briefness, the card spoke volumes. I was *dear* to someone whom I loved, and no matter what the outcome was regarding the cottage, that love would never change. It was the simplest message a person could hope to understand, and how wonderful it was; unconditional love. It was the greatest triumph in life, and as I reread the sentiments, I felt a warm rush of emotion in my mind, body and spirit. What more could anyone want? Unconditional love.

I stood the card up on the wooden table, went upstairs to bed, and, with a smile on my face and a burden off my chest, was asleep within minutes.

MONDAY

1.

I slept in peace the entire night, the dreams I had were dreams of the people who had always been a part of this place. My dreams were filled with happiness and joy, and the only thing better than dreaming of these people was awakening to know that these people were in my life even while I was awake. Bella was there of course, her son Alex, my wife Susan and son, Antony. My parents and sister had visited me throughout the night, and both grandparents joined with Aunt Josie and Theresa, as well as both twins. My dreams had been reunions, and surrounded here with love and familiarity I knew nothing less was possible.

The day was cold and the sun was bright, but I just lay there on the bed daydreaming of family and Bella's visit. Her visit with me here at this time would become yet another memory that would be stored forever within these walls. I thought about my flight tomorrow from Bradley International Airport at three in the afternoon back to Florida. I had the whole day today to myself, a day I could actually sit back and enjoy this magnificent place again for the first time. I was starting anew.

Sure, I had to tell the broker that I would not be selling the cottage, and I had to let Susan know that we'd probably have to get a second mortgage on our house to pay off those that had voted to sell, but I felt overcome with joy that this place would still exist throughout my lifetime, and be right here, safely where it belonged.

In a moment of true euphoria, I laughed out loud and smiled, thanking God for the opportunity to continue something so beautiful that had been started oh so long ago, and could now continue on. This cottage and all its memories encompassed so much and was so important to so very many people that my laugh filled the whole cottage, a 'HA' that my grandfather would have been proud to hear! As I placed my head up on the pillow and caught glimpses of the ocean, I imagined new reunions and visits to this place of wonder, new generations of children brought here to bond in ways that only family can. There were new memories to be made, and new pictures would be added to albums already bursting from the love and laughter they contained. Everything somehow just felt right again, everything was how it should be. Life as I knew it was good and the past and the present would continue to blend seamlessly into the future.

FINIS

Made in the USA
Columbia, SC
17 March 2025

55226213R00161